the FEVER

DARK

A TOUCHSTONE BOOK
Published by Simon & Schuster
New York London Toronto Sydney

TOUCHSTONE
Rockefeller Center
1230 Avenue of the Americas
New York, NY 10020

Designed by Jaime Putorti

Manufactured in the United States of America

10   9   8   7   6   5   4   3   2   1

Library of Congress Cataloging-in-Publication Data is available

ISBN-13: 978-0-7432-7237-7
ISBN-10:   0-7432-7237-4

For information regarding special discounts for bulk purchases,
please contact Simon & Schuster Special Sales at 1-800-456-6798
or business@simonandschuster.com.

the FEVER

Introduction

If sex is the ultimate drug, then soul singers are the perfect aphrodisiac. Sure, Frank Sinatra wet some panties back in his day, but no one makes a person's nature rise like a sweet-sounding, please-baby-please, got-to-give-it-up, you're-all-I-need-to-get-by soul man.

At first he is unknown to us. The brother could be a burly country kid, a city-bred slicker, or a quiet church boy. He emerges from the heart of the black community with a message of desire. His ability to sing out our collective lust transforms him into a secular god. Soon we know them by their first names—Sam, Smokey, Otis, Marvin, Teddy, Luther. This new generation? Maxwell, D'Angelo, and Usher? They just cut to the chase.

We, the fans, worship at their altars. Shower them with money and fame. In return, they bless us with sensual sounds that unlock our libidos. You can't truly embody carnal desire unless you allow it to enter your soul. You have to eat lust like a communal wafer. I know all this because I am a high priest in this religion. I have inducted scores into the secular sect of sonic seduction.

For many years I have journeyed across this country in search of young soul disciples to teach the rituals of public erotica. Ultimately the instruction became more than a course of education. It grew inside them. It became a kind of infection I like to call the Fever. This Fever is not some benign, three-day cold you can knock out with orange juice and aspirin. Once overcome by the Fever, it penetrates your DNA and alters your cell structure. Your sex appeal goes off the charts. Young girls scream. Adult women swoon. Even grandmothers get embarrassed by their sticky wet dreams.

Sure, the transformation is amazing, but that doesn't mean it's all good. Once acquired, the Fever takes on a life of its own. Sex happens everywhere, all the time, until it loses meaning. You become insatiable and then the Fever consumes you. Wears out your body 'cause too much fucking is like too much herb, too much candy, and too much food—it has nasty consequences.

The Fever is what got Sam Cooke shot at a tacky L.A. motel. The Fever got Teddy Pendergrass crippled in a car accident. Because of the Fever, Eric Benet couldn't keep

Halle. The Fever got Michael Jackson catching a case over some underage boy. The Fever got R. Kelly on film with an underage girl.

I was in the music game for almost thirty years and I've seen a lot in that time. Bold-faced names doing plenty of Fever-induced dirt. In various capacities—manager, publicist, media trainer, flunky, pimp—I have covered it all up. I've stood just outside the frame of many *People* magazine photos. I'm the person slipping *ET* the right questions and vetoing the wrong ones. I'm the one who tells Page Six "no comment" when I damn well have something to say, but too much class to say it.

Since the late seventies right up till last year, I managed a stable of love men who enjoyed hit records and sold out concert halls full of screaming women nationwide. And every last one of them, sooner or later, was overcome by the Fever. For a long time, I held back from telling tales out of school. It's tacky. It's bad form. It can get you hurt. It can hurt a lot of people. But now the record industry is in the toilet. Downloading has replaced record buying. Counterfeit CDs burned on PCs sound as good as those from the factories. Kids are playing the Xbox more than buying CD singles. Shit, Grand Theft Auto is bigger than *Thriller*.

When I was first got in this game there were six major labels and at least twenty or so aggressive independent companies that could sneak up and have a hit record. Now almost all the indies have disappeared into multinational ledger books and the few remaining majors are run by pencil necks who couldn't recognize a hit if it was done with a gun. Belt tightening rules the day, which means much less paper for an old dog like me.

So what you're reading is an experiment in tabloid capitalism. I saw how Superhead got paid over her "confessions." Now's a chance to see if the world is ready to understand the Fever. And if I can stack a little paper off my tale? Well, that's not a bad thing.

What I'm gonna do is tell one story from midway in my career, back when I was working with a young singer I'll call Brian Barnes—"BB" or "Brain" to friends and lovers. This is a story about how music + money + celebrity = sex and always will.

Does this story have a moral? Well, maybe. The story I'm about to tell clearly shows that sex corrupts as absolutely as power and as profoundly as money. Once a man has seen women give themselves freely, night after night, his perspective on love is altered and it never comes all the way back to "normal." Sex hits you as quickly as coke and hangs on like heroin. But there is no methadone for sex addiction. You can try your hand at going cold turkey on sex (yeah, right), but to be normal is to be horny and to be horny is to wanna fuck and to wanna fuck can lead you back to the Fever, like it is the goddamn yellow brick road.

• • •

In 1990 Brian Barnes was a young singer with a fine voice, quiet confidence, and a bright future. He was part of the new jack swing sweepstakes in which Keith Sweat, Guy's Aaron Hall, Johnny Kemp, Bobby Brown, and a few other voices battled to become the leading love man of the nineties. His voice was a little bit Marvin Gaye with a touch of Frankie Beverly. He went from a taste of child stardom to competing in amateur night shows to boldly tossing his hotel room key into the audience of screaming young women. This young brother went from the outhouse to the penthouse in one crazy summer.

It was, of course, owing to a hit record that sent him on a quick tour from Philly to D.C., from ATL to the Big Easy, to Chitown and all the way to the City of Angels. Money was made, but the fucking was the real focus. Groupies and starlets, newswomen and hotel staff, parking lot attendants and KFC cashiers. They all participated in our Olympics. Yes, ours. Though they were all looking for a piece of Brian Barnes, I made myself available and found heaven in my lap night after night.

As Brian became more famous, he became more feverish. And by the next year, he had flamed out like a match dropped in water. In his case, the flame didn't just burn the match. It consumed the whole damn box.

chapter 1
Maggie Was Plush

Back in April 1990 I was working in New York City for Plush Management, a company that, as the name suggests, worked with upscale pop acts whose music was not too gritty, not too nasty, and not at all urban. But in light of the megastardom of Prince, Michael Jackson, Lionel Richie, etc., plus the growing popularity of rap, Plush realized they needed to get into the black music game, so they sought me out. I'd agreed to hook up with Plush because my recent divorce (and subsequent outsize alimony settlement) required a regular cash flow to keep me solvent. I was thirty-two years old and, at that point, had been in the business about fifteen busy years. I'd made money, had several jobs in corporate musical chairs, and been bounced around enough that I was no longer bright-eyed and bushy-tailed. I'd become a "road dog," aka a dude who felt most alive traveling on tour buses, checking into hotels, and being backstage at concert halls. I got real antsy sitting in my home in St. Albans, Queens (which is what ultimately destroyed by marriage).

Plush's corporate culture wasn't quite ready for rap yet. They talked the talk, but every time I brought in an MC I thought had potential folks got cold feet. Not that I loved rap music myself, but I realized black music was always evolving. In the black music world, to cling to the past was to get left behind—be it when funk replaced R&B or when disco replaced funk. You had to roll with the musical punches or get pushed to the sidelines.

"New jack swing," driven by Teddy Riley's big beat production, was the new wave rocking the charts. It was a hip-hopped version of R&B with enough melody to satisfy older heads, and I'd convinced Plush's powers that, unlike rap, such an act would fit snuggly with Plush. The "power" running Plush was a woman named Maggie May, a peroxide blonde who'd begun her career as a personal assistant to the Rolling Stones' manager during one of their legendary mid-seventies jaunts around the U.S.

Maggie still had a rock groupie's taste for too much foundation and lots of black eyeliner. For Maggie, age wasn't nothing but a number. She had to be at least fifty, but that didn't stop her from wearing short skirts, strappy

heels, and bosom-revealing blouses that made her a favorite dinner companion of high-level record executives
and aging rock stars. I'd once heard an older white man
at a record-listening party tell another, "Dude, she used
to have the best ass in the business."

Though time had taken its toil on that ass (and other
body parts), Maggie still carried herself like a fox and,
because she did, the lady retained a palpable air of sexuality. So I enjoyed our little private meetings. Maggie
would always sit on the edge of her desk with her thin
pale legs crossing and uncrossing for my (and her)
amusement. Sometimes right in the middle of a meeting
I'd fantasize about screwing her on that desk, with Mick
Jagger watching and applauding my fine work.

"Dark? Are you daydreaming on my time?" Maggie
teased as my eyes drifted too far up her thigh.

"No," I said with a smile. "What I was thinking . . .
with Whitney Houston as romantic lead opposite a big
white male movie star, LL Cool J walking around *Satur-
day Night Live* with his shirt off, it's time to strike. We
need to sign a client we can sell in the ghetto and still get
his picture in every white girl's suburban high school
locker. That's the way the culture's going and Plush
should be right there on that edge."

"Okay," Maggie said. "Find me a guy who can sing
and can make the ladies scream and I'll put the full re-
sources of Plush behind him and, of course, behind you.
As you know, this rap thing hasn't been a good fit for

Plush, but a sexy young chocolate singer, that I can understand."

"I bet," I joked, and we both laughed.

"Dark," she then said, "I want him to be like you."

"And what does that mean?" I replied defensively.

"I see how you move. How you look at the secretaries here. How you stand next to the ladies in this office and at parties. You are always on the prowl. I want you to find and/or groom a singer to have those qualities. If you can get a good-looking young man to project that in his voice and his movements onstage, I believe we can sell more records than Michael Jackson."

"You're probably right," I replied.

Maggie uncrossed her legs, giving me a clear view of her black lace panties. "Find us that singer, Dark, and I'll finance a full-on black music department here."

"I see—I mean, I hear you." We both laughed again. Then I got up, gave her a kiss on the cheek, and headed out to find America's next black sex symbol.

chapter 2
Chi Chi Knows

I needed a sexy, strong singing black man in his twenties who didn't yet have a record deal and who'd do precisely what I told him to. The first step involved doing something no one in the record biz liked to do: I actually listened to the unsolicited tapes and DATs—aka the slush pile—submitted to Plush by inexperienced, unsigned acts trying to strike gold (or perhaps platinum).

We literally received scores of such tapes on a daily basis, usually accompanied by a head shot, a bio, and some crudely put-together amateur music video. Today there's less physical slush since these unsolicited submissions now come in via the Internet. But back in prehistoric 1990 the pile of unlistened-to tapes could have filled broom closets. Generally you didn't listen to unsolicited tapes for fear of any number of potential lawsuits—we stole their songs being accusation number one. If there was no self-addressed stamped envelope with the package, the tapes were tossed.

But I was a man with a mission, even if that required spending one long afternoon trolling for gold amid the slush pile. Since Plush was known for rock and pop we didn't get that many R&B vocal submissions. The ones we did receive fell into two groups: group one, pretty boys who couldn't sing at all or those of moderate ability who aspired to be the next Al B. "Nite and Day" Sure!; group two, big-voiced gospel-bred types who were either overweight, uninteresting, looked gay, or all three. Not a keeper in the bunch. The slush pile lived up to its name.

On to plan B, which was, potentially, a lot more fun. There was a Keith Sweat video shoot at Cheetah, a club in the Twenties off Broadway. They were using a lot of hot video girl dancers, including an old fuck buddy, so I rolled there, reasoning it took a fine girl to identify a fly guy.

It was typical performance video: screaming crowd, lots of smoke, and guys in hi-top fades. In the style of the time, the dancers were wearing backwards baseball caps, hockey jerseys, and their moves were more athletic than the hoochie moves of today. These dancers were more Michael Jackson-meets-body-popping than stripper chic. And the best of the bunch was Chi Chi, a lean, bronze goddess with Native American cheekbones and a strong redbone undertone to her skin. Chi Chi was no typical shortie—at five foot eleven, Chi Chi could intimidate a weak-willed man and straight up squash a punk. Her eyes were long and almond shaped, and when she surveyed a man they got thin like slits. They were eyes that could make you question everything about yourself, so you didn't step to Chi Chi if you couldn't come correct. Not surprisingly Chi Chi was a demanding lover. When (and if) you satisfied Chi Chi, you knew you'd thrown the fuck down.

The dancers were chilling in a temporary trailer in a parking lot next to Cheetah. When the assistant director called for lunch break I headed over there. A burly production assistant with headphones around his large peanut head eyed me suspiciously as I rolled up.

"Yeah?" he said, trying to sound tough.

"I'm here to see Chi Chi," I said and handed him my business card.

"Is she expecting you?"

"No. I just stopped by the shoot and wanted to say hello."

He eyed the card and then handed it back to me. "Well," he replied, "I can't help you. I can't go in there. You'll just have to wait for her to come out."

"What? You can't knock on the door?"

"I know my job," he said with unnecessary hostility. Obviously a jealous-hearted sucka. I was trying to surprise Chi Chi but now I had to call. Without another word to him I pulled out my cell and dialed her.

"Hey, it's Dark. I'm standing outside. You need to come out here and get with me."

The trailer door swung open and Chi Chi stood with one hand holding her cell and the other on her hip. A New York Rangers hockey jersey hung loosely from her shoulders. Into the cell she said, "Some brothers have good timing and some brothers don't."

Putting away my cell I asked, "Which am I?"

"TBD, Dark. To be determined."

"Can I come in?"

"C'mon."

The burly PA cut in. "I was told not to let anyone in."

Chi Chi looked at him sideways. "That's right. People we don't want in here, you don't let in. But this is my future baby daddy, so he's coming in. Ya hear me?"

I smiled at the PA and walked up the steps into the trailer. Chi Chi gave me a soft kiss on the lips and let me enter. There were no other girls in the trailer, but plenty of evidence they'd been there—makeup cases, fashion magazines, a bra or two, and the sticky scent of sweat and perfume. I cleared off some space and sat on a sofa, while Chi Chi sat across from me in a makeup chair. She was barefoot, so when she crossed her long, well-muscled legs I just gazed at her fine, lanky bronze limbs intertwined from her toes to her thigh. She looked at me and said, "I know you want something."

"To see you, of course."

Chi Chi snorted out a laugh. "You have my cell, pager, and home numbers. If you just wanted to hang out, you'd use one of them. You need a flavor, you come see me. You might even think you could get some spur-of-the-moment ass. Am I wrong?"

"Not totally."

"Yup. You record biz niggas are about two degrees above drug dealers on the food chain of men. But with a dealer at least I know he's trying to get you hooked. You record biz guys have so many angles it's hard to keep up."

"So," I said with a smirk, "how's Keith Sweat?" Word on the street was that she was sleeping with the new jack swinger.

"About as good as the three hos I hear you're sleeping with since your girl kicked you to the curb."

"Three? I have to check. It may be more than that."

"Dark, you talk like you got a big dick."

"I think you know."

She leaned forward and said, "It depends on how you define 'big.' "

I laughed at that. If you let her, Chi Chi would break you down so low you wouldn't be sitting on the tops of your shoes.

"Big, baby," I said. Then I unzipped by pants and pulled out my dick and let it plop against the sofa. "Looks like this."

She burst out laughing. "You are crazier than I remember, Dark!"

"Is that so? Well, show me how crazy you are. Show me yours."

"You a fool," she said. "Acting like you ten years old."

I replied, "C'mon, Chi Chi," and took my dick in my right hand and began playing with it, moving my fingers slowly around the shaft.

"The other dancers could come in here at any time," she said. She'd seen my dick before—it was nothing new to her—but I could tell she was turned on by me acting so bold.

"Ain't like they ain't seen it before."

Chi Chi's eyes became slits as she watched my dick thicken and expand.

"But it never gets old, does it?" I said with a smile. Then I added, "Take you clothes off."

"Make me," she said.

I stood up, walked over to he, and pulled her hockey jersey over her head till it was off.

Chi Chi was wearing a bright red bra, an earring loop in her belly button, and matching red panties. "These are," she said, "my lucky dancing panties and bra."

"Lucky me," I replied. I took my hand off my dick and, without using my hands, moved it up and down, as if by a lever. It was a trick I'd mastered one night when I was fourteen. It never failed to amuse females.

"Oh, tricks now, huh?" Chi Chi popped out one of her

small pointy titties and bent her neck down. I knew what was coming next. Homegirl had a long-ass tongue. And there it went, sliding smoothly out of her mouth and moistening that black pointy nipple.

"I remember that tongue."

"Yeah," she said. "And I remember that clever dick of yours."

I stepped back to the sofa and pulled my pants down around my ankles. I pulled out my favorite brand of condoms, Trojans extra large in the green-and-white package, and slid one on.

"Come over here."

"Am I supposed to be that easy?"

"For me? Hell yeah. Bring that sweet pussy over here."

I guess Chi Chi liked my tone 'cause she slid off her panties, strutted over to the sofa, and slid that pussy right down on my dick. She slid onto me with a loud groan, and then settled in atop me like a jockey. She rode me hard as her pointy-ass nipples bounced in and out of my mouth. Chi Chi was a loud gal who liked to moan. I smiled as I thought of that burly PA sucka hearing me fuck this fine-ass woman he was allegedly protecting.

My thoughts got refocused when Chi Chi arched her back, bending her body away from me and pulling on my dick with her pussy, gripping me like a joystick. She controlled the tempo with her thighs, grinding me down like corn meal. In between breaths she asked, "Okay, what else do you want, Dark?"

I squeezed out, "Is this the right time?"

"Come on, Dark," she said as she bent back hard, "I know you can do more than one thing at a time."

"I need," I said between breaths, as she pumped harder, "I need a singer. A star. Someone I can manage."

"That's easy. You should have just asked."

"Yeah, right." I could feel my body building to a major orgasm. There was pressure coming up from between my balls and anus.

"Brian . . . Barnes," she said breathlessly.

"What?"

"Brian Barnes. He'll be at Amateur Night at the Apollo tomorrow."

"Okay," I moaned, desperately trying to hold on. "I got it."

"Yeah, Dark. I can tell you almost do."

"Yeah." A white rush swooped through my dick.

"And I get a piece of the deal, right?"

I was about to burst. "Hell yeah!" I said, and then howled like a werewolf at a bright full moon and fell back against the sofa, spent like an ejected bullet.

There was a knock on the door. The burly PA yelled, "Chi Chi, you're wanted on the set."

"Tell them I'll be out in ten minutes." Chi Chi dismounted me without another word and then walked into a restroom in the back. I tried to pull myself together, but

Chi Chi's wetness was all over me, like I'd taken a bath in her body's juices. I must have dozed, because what I remember next is Chi Chi's long, red tongue dancing across my lips. I awakened to her standing in front of me, hockey jersey back on, a baseball cap pulled over her eyes.

"Remember what you promised," she said. "Two points and a ten-thousand-dollar finders fee."

"Did I agree to that?"

"Oh yeah. You definitely did. Trust me, the boy's a star. He's young, though. Put him with a corrupt brother like you and who knows what hell he'll raise."

"You slept with him?"

"A boy like that you sample, but you don't give them the whole show. They have to be worthy of that."

"I'm flattered."

"Be flattered. And don't try to fuck me on the deal."

Again the burly PA knocked on the door. Chi Chi took my arm and escorted me out of the trailer and over to Cheetah. I could feel the PA's eyes shooting daggers at my back, but I didn't care. Chi Chi had given me a tip and she was a damn good judge of male talent. At Cheetah's front door I leaned over to kiss her, but she turned her head, placing my lips on her cheek.

"Keith might get jealous," she explained.

"No, we wouldn't want that."

"I'll let Brian know you're coming. 'Bye, partner."

chapter 3
Brian Barnes and
Secret Sushi

I'd been going to the Apollo Theater since back when James Brown could still do his splits and had spied plenty of top-notch talent grace its ancient stage on Amateur Night. So I was prepared to be blown away by Brian Barnes, but I wasn't. Neither was the crowd, which picked him second to a cute quartet of adolescent singer/MCs who bit the doo-wop/hip-hop style of Staten Island's Force MDs.

Barnes was good, but he had a long way to go to be truly great. A thin, light brown kid with a well-maintained hi-top fade, a see-through black mesh shirt, and Hammer-like genie pants, Barnes's styling was cheap and absolutely wack, which did not endear him to the Apollo's picky faithful. Equally disappointing was that Barnes didn't move fluidly, either. Not totally stiff, but no Michael Jackson, either. He just didn't have it dynamic enough going on to top a singing and dancing quintet of cute black kiddies.

But don't get me wrong, I saw more good than bad in Barnes that night. Chi Chi was right—the kid had something. He didn't exude charisma, yet he was very watchable. He did generate a few whoops from the paying customers and incited a few girls to stand up and sway. A petite Japanese woman in a Gucci jacket had leapt out of her orchestra seat and strolled up to the lip of the famous stage to roll her hips as Barnes sang. Plus I loved his choice of cover song: Marvin Gaye's "After the Dance," a truly sensual song from the romantic masterpiece *I Want You* album. His take on it preserved some of the feel of the original, but then he uptempoed the last section, giving it a more contemporary feel than Marvin's original. This idiosyncratic, smart choice of material and its interpretation is what really sold me on Brian Barnes. He already understood something about how to make sensual music and that was a key part of this game.

I ventured backstage at the old theater and then walked down some stairs into the inner bowels under the stage where, for decades, stars and wannabes alike had walked. In that waiting area under the stage, a place where the Temptations had practiced dance moves with choreographer Cholly Atkins in front of the long mirror and Aretha Franklin had rehearsed with her background singers, there was a table set up with sodas and finger food. There I found Brian foraging through a bowl of stale potato chips. His fade was fading. Perspiration made his forehead shine. A funky aroma emanated from under his underarms.

I ignored the scent and focused on his smooth, light brown unblemished skin and prominent cheekbones. He had full but not too thick lips and, with teeth in good shape, a really striking smile. He'd photograph well. All I'd have to do was polish this little diamond so he gleamed.

"Hello, Brian," I said. "My name is Dark. I enjoyed your performance very much."

"Cool, man. Nice to meet you. Chi Chi left me a message that you might stop by."

"How do you know her?" I asked. I wanted to see how he'd talk about a sexy woman. Would he leer or be chill?

"An ex-girlfriend used to dance for her and she gave Chi Chi my tape. She's been a supporter ever since. She always said when the right opportunity came along she'd hook me up." Brian played it straight, sounded like he wasn't intimidated by a beautiful woman. That was a good sign.

"Well, Chi Chi is true to her word," I said. "Not to hype you, but I'm the right opportunity."

"Oh yeah?" Brian said with a skeptical smile. "You 'bout to change my life?"

"Nah. Just enhance it enough so that we can both get paid."

I could tell he was surprised that I was so forward, but I didn't have time to be coy. Brian had the raw materials. He needed to know I was the man to make him a commodity.

A very comely, short, brown-skinned sister with a kind, round face walked over and gave Brian a hug and kiss. "Mr. Dark, this is Benita Wall."

To which she added possessively, "I'm his girlfriend." Brian didn't contradict her, though I observed she didn't wait for him to volunteer those words.

"Baby," Barnes said, "I didn't think you'd make it tonight."

"I'm going into the hospital later," she said. Then she raised up the towel in her hands and wiped his brow. "When you told me Mr. Dark was coming to see you I felt I should be here. I know your dancer friend said he was an important man so, you know, I thought I should be here to support you."

"That's sweet," her boyfriend replied.

My translation: Benita wanted to see who that chickenhead Chi Chi had sent to see her man. If I was Barnes's girlfriend I'd be suspicious of anything Chi Chi was involved in, too. I could see immediately she was a potential adversary in the battle to obtain Brian Barnes.

I just said, "It sure is," and forced a smile. "You're a doctor?"

"No," she said regretfully. "I'm a nurse at Downstate in Brooklyn. But I love helping people, whether it be a patient or my man."

"I hear that," I said as I surveyed her.

After he changed clothes Brian, Benita, and I walked over to Sylvia's for a soul food–supported getting-to-know-you session. His background story started off as I'd expected: born and raised in the projects on St. Nicholas in the 130s by a unwed mother; sang at White Rock Baptist Church as a little kid; at one point contemplated becoming a minister. At fourteen he was recruited into a Jackson Five imitation group called Five that cut a few singles for a black gangster-owned label called Council Records (dope king-pin Nicky Barnes—no relation to Brian—owned a piece from jail). The kiddie quintet played around the tristate area, even opening for Run-DMC in Trenton, New Jersey—a personal highlight for Brian. But they never made any national noise and barely made a dime.

"Five went nowhere," he recalled ruefully, "but I lost any stage fright I had. I know I'm not the best singer in the world, but I also know how to bring a song across—you saw that tonight. I get myself some good material and a hot video, I know I can sell records." Confident but realistic, which was better than the usual neophyte attitude of arrogance and naïveté.

"So," I asked Brian, "how long have you two been together?"

"About two years now." Though I was looking at Brian, Benita had jumped in. "We've wanted to move in together, but the places we've seen had either been too expensive or not quite right."

I glanced back over at Brian, who shrugged his shoulders, and added, "We're not in too much of a rush, though. We'll find the right place in time."

"Yeah," I agreed, "there's time. But you know, a singing career can be hard on a relationship. All that time away from home. Are you ready for that, Benita?"

She replied in a very firm tone. "If it doesn't happen soon Brian can go back to school. Start at a community college and get a business degree. There's more to him than singing. So I feel like we have a good backup plan."

"Yeah," Brian said, supporting her with his words but not his body language. He'd do it if he had to, but having a business was not his dream.

"Yeah, I feel you," I replied. "It's always good to have a backup plan. A music career is a gamble. But if you win you can make more money than you would in three lifetimes of nine to five. It's a gamble, but it's a bold one."

"But how long can you chase that dream? At some point you have to get on with the rest of your life," she said.

"I see where you're coming from," I said diplomatically.

Brian just sat there and took a sip of iced tea. I got the feeling this was a conversation Brian and Benita had been having for a while. She glanced down at her watch and then announced, "I have to head off to Brooklyn."

"It was a pleasure to meet you," I said.

"Likewise." She stood up, paused, and then said to Brian, "Baby, you gonna walk me outside?"

"Sure." He jumped up. "Dark, I'll be right back." If Brian Barnes was gonna be a nine-to-five guy, dreaming of two kids and a home in the suburbs, he had excellent wife material. But if he was hungry to be ghetto fabulous, then he was destined to break Benita's heart. And, if things worked out between Brian and me, I'd help him do it. Not that I was a home wrecker, but Brian needed to be in aggressive, get-pussy mode while we were recording. I didn't want him content sounding or, even worse, being pussy whipped. I wanted him sounding like a stud. You could feel that on a record.

Brian returned in about fifteen minutes and we did a little more chatting to tie things up. While we were waiting on the bill, a group of about thirty Japanese tourists entered the dining room led by a guide with a clipboard. A busload came to Sylvia's after Amateur Night every Wednesday. They'd get a full night of Negrophilia—singing, dancing, and collard greens. Brian and I were equally amused by the orderly line and ubiquitous cameras when two of the Japanese girls approached our table. Both were stylishly and expensively dressed. Designer brands covered every part of their thin little bodies; both hovered just below five feet and had small breasts on their otherwise boyish shapes. They each sported thick brown bangs and pageboys, round moon-shaped faces, and beautiful, long, curly eyelashes that were enthusiastically batting at Brian. The slightly cuter one bubbled with excitement about Amateur Night in general and Brian's performance in particular in heavily accented English. Her name was Yuko and it was she who'd run up to the edge of the stage to dance.

Even before Yuko and her girlfriend Suzi asked for an autograph, I offered to photograph them with Brian, knowing a Japanese without a camera is damn near a Korean. So I took cameras from both women and placed them cheek to smiling cheek with Brian, much to their giggling pleasure and his slight embarrassment. Did he not like Japanese girls? Personally, I never much went for Japanese girls myself. If I went Asian at all it had to be a Korean since they tended to be bigger boned and more curvaceous than Japanese women. Still, this provided a golden opportunity to get some insight into my potential new client. If Brian was gonna be my sex symbol, I needed to see how he flexed his predatory instincts.

Turned out the girls had just moved to New York from Tokyo, part of the wave of Japanese kids taking advantage of the extremely favorable exchange rate for the yen in the 1990s. It was dirt cheap for two well-paid bank employees to relocate here in search of adventure.

"We love the passion and beauty of black people," Yuko said earnestly. My translation: We're interested in getting busy with tall black men. The streets of New York were then teeming with short cute Japanese women walking around with the trendiest designer bags on one arm and a brother, often a swaggering b-boy, on the other.

I asked, "You guys interested in going to a Harlem club?" They nodded and smiled.

"Yo, Dark, man, I don't know," Brian said. There was a quiver in his voice, like he wanted to be bad, but couldn't admit it.

"Come on, Brian. We need to bond and this would be a good way to do it." I cut him a look that said, Let's do these girls, and he smiled nervously. He wanted to do it, but loyalty to Benita was holding him back. Quite honorable, of course, but not what I was looking for.

We went up to Well's, a venerable jazz club/restaurant that used to be up in the 140s. The place had seen better days, but Wynton Marsalis and other current jazz gods still rolled through to jam and indulge in their legendary dinners of chicken and waffles. The four of us chilled in a back booth with a clear view of the stage. I didn't recognize any of the players, but whoever these brothers were, they could blow. The Japanese, as the stereotype went, loved jazz more than black folks; Yuko and Suzi lived up to the hype. Yuko got up and started doing a wild interpretative jazz dance—something that

Eartha Kitt might have performed while playing Cat-woman back in the day. As the brothers grooved through a fierce version of Lionel Hampton's "Flying Home," she grinded her tiny hips and twisted her little hands before Brian.

Things got hotter when Suzi, who seemed quite shy at first, slid out of her seat and into the aisle alongside Yuko. It wasn't mechanical like two strippers rubbing up against each other for dollars bills, but totally abandoned and unselfconscious. That's really attractive in one woman and quite thrilling in two. Heads at the bar turned. Our waitress, a sister in her forties, sucked her teeth 'cause she could sense how this was gonna go down. A couple of older black men in suits sipped their Jack Daniels' with quiet amusement. And Brian Barnes, the prime audience for this unexpected show, looked embarrassed and excited, humiliated and aroused all at once.

"Ladies," he said, "please sit down."

"This dance is for you, Brian," Yuko said. "In honor of your voice."

"Cool," he said, "I am honored. But please come over here and sit next to me."

And so, to the disappointment of many inside Well's, the girls sat back down. I was a little disappointed with Brian's reaction—guess he wasn't much of an off-stage extrovert—until I noticed his left hand moving slowly under the table and Yuko leaning back with her eyes closed. Trying not to be obvious, I leaned sideways and could glimpse Brian's hand moving around under Yuko's little dress. Yuko's right hand begin to move in a small circular motion, as well. To my surprise this little lady had unzipped Brian's pants and slid his penis out of his blue-and-white boxers. Now, Brian didn't have the biggest dick I've ever seen on a brother, but in Yuko's little palm it lived large. This was multiculturalism of the highest order—a black singer and a Japanese banker masturbating each other to the syncopations of a Harlem jazz band.

I don't know if he came or not, but as soon as there was a lull in the music, Brian suggested we break out. I had a sedan waiting outside and offered him a ride home. Instead he opted to take a gypsy cab. He did, however, pull Yuko over for some quiet talk before leaving.

"I'll make sure they get home," I assured him. "And I'll call you tomorrow and set up a meeting with my lawyer."

"You're serious, huh?" he asked nervously.

"I saw what I needed to see tonight, Brian. We're gonna do business."

I gave him a hug and then piled my two new Japanese friends into the sedan. On the way downtown I grilled them about Brian: both girls thought he was sexy and a fine singer ("Like the great Michael Jackson"), though they both thought he could be better dressed. Suzi, who apparently had been inspired by her jazz dance, suggested we hit a karaoke bar in the East Village. Then she snuggled up to me and said something to Yuko in Japanese that made them both laugh. Cool, I thought, maybe I will have some sushi tonight.

The spot was in the basement of a nondescript building near Astor Place and marked with only one blue light. If you didn't know it was there, you'd never notice it and, let me tell you, you'd be missing out. It was dark and comfy, with room after room filled with saki-swilling, well-dressed Japanese men and women either singing pop tunes poorly or sitting in banquets laughing and smoking away.

We fell in with a group of their friends—mostly giddy, chatty girls knocking back saki like it was tap water. Most of this crew had a limited command of English, but were equally cute and trendy in their wardrobe. Suzi, who was now all over me, holding my waist and cradling my head in her little hands, got up and sang a highly accented version of "Let's Get It On," so loose and off-key it made me laugh. I got up and did Teddy Pendergrass's "Love TKO" and the girls squealed as I rolled my hips and shouted Teddy Bear style.

The Japanese have a very practical culture, one that accommodates desire and excess as much as tradition and honor. Which is why there were several private party rooms set up in the back of this Japanese-owned club, for post-singing personal celebrations. I watched as Suzi and Yuko negotiated with a hard-ass manager who cut me a dirty look as the girls tried to rent a room. He wasn't crazy about letting a black dick loose in his hen house, but Yuko and Suzi were damned persistent. After much haggling, it cost me three hundred dollars to get a private room, but it would prove to be money well spent.

As befitting the tiny stature of the place's regular customers, the room was small and narrow, sort of the size of a sexy jail cell. But unlike the state pen, there was jasmine incense burning, a neatly made-up bed, complimentary saki, a shower stall, and three small TV screens built in the walls that broadcast the karaoke performances sans sound. The sound of a traditional Japanese melody played on flute and some stringed instrument played quietly.

Suzi sat me on the bed, slowly opening my shirt, pulling off my sweater, sliding off my slacks and white boxers, and rolling down my socks until all I had on was my Rolex and a diamond pinky ring. After neatly folding my clothes onto a low chair, Suzi turned on the shower and guided me in. As I washed my body with a soapy sponge, Suzi slowly undressed herself, watching me wash as I watched her disrobe. When she squeezed into the shower with me, Suzi rubbed my back and buttocks with the sponge and then gave me the sponge to scrub her bony yellow body. As I washed her I took inventory of her tight little package: two dark nipples, both upturned and perky; a small belly with an out-y belly button; short, thin, black pubic hair that matched the pageboy haircut on her now wet head. After setting this up she seemed nervous, perhaps a little intimidated by my nakedness. I used my signature up-and-down dick move ("Look, no hands!") to relax her a bit which made her giggle.

After the shower we wiped each other down with jasmine-scented towels, exploring all the ridges and cervices of each other's bodies. We sat on the bed, exploring our bodies with our hands, like two blind lovers, thrilling to the taunt muscles and soft curves and surfaces of the other. I picked up her short legs and rubbed them in my hands. Then I raised her legs up and bent them at the knee so I could suck her small, slightly soapy-tasting toes. I slid them in and out of my mouth. Suzi moaned so loudly I thought her G-spot was in her left big toe.

As my tongue slid between her toes one of my hands found her pussy, where I felt thin, soft pubic hair and the sticky moisture of arousal. She pulled a condom from under the bed and put her feet on the floor. I took it from her and rolled it down myself. She started going down on me but I can be a little impatient with head. When I get real hard, head can't move me as deeply as intercourse. So I pulled her head up, kissed her deeply—tasting a weird blend of condom rubber and saki—and then placed her in my lap, facing away from me. As my dick entered her Suzi made the sound of a hissing cat, which was sexy and slightly scary, too. She slid down on me and suddenly her body quivered with an orgasm before she was even halfway down. Suzi was a wild mix of decorum and intensity that was making me rethink my views of Japanese women.

In fact my mind was totally changed when I finally noticed that Yuko, apparently still horny from Brian (and very comfortable seeing Suzi naked), was standing inside the door with one hand squeezing a nipple and the other moving busily inside her pussy. It made me pump Suzi faster as I watched Yuko and Yuko watched Suzi and me.

I came in a huge, rolling surge that rolled down my spine, down my ass, and right up out of my dick. It felt like a volcano. I flopped back on the bed and out of Suzi's pussy. Suzi and Yuko came over to my body with wet hand towels and began wiping the sweat off my body, like I was a slightly grimy house that needed cleansing. The unexpected attention of four hands washing over my chest, arms, and legs quickly got the attention of my dick, which regained strength. Soon both these women were on either side of me—their pussies pink and moist with my fingers in them—as they used their fingers and mouths on me and on each other. As this sensual exchange went on I looked at the video screens and saw scores of Japanese singing soul songs with saki-fueled fury.

As I laid my head back and breathed deeply, my mind sadly wandered back to work: How do I get rid of Brian Barnes's girlfriend?

chapter 4
Yoli and the
Night of Toes

Instead of doing a showcase gig with Brian at a club where I had to worry about hustling ticket sales, hecklers, and bad sound, I booked SIR, an equipment rental and rehearsal space then in the West Fifties. SIR was convenient for record executives since all their offices were in midtown, so they had no reason not to show up. The downside was that Brian would be performing without the benefit of horny Japanese girls or energetic Apollo customers. I worried that Brian's style might seem too raw to a cold, critical record executive. After all, their job was mostly seeing flaws to justify saying no. So all that day of the showcase I worried and fretted. I didn't verbalize my concerns to Brain, but when he showed up for soundcheck he must have felt my anxiety.

"It's gonna be good, Dark," he said. "I'm ready."

"I know," I said, lying a little. "But don't you have any female friends you wanna invite? Just two or three, tops. You know, like your girlfriend and a few more. Some demonstrative females, okay?"

"My girl is real quiet. But I'll talk to my sister. She's kinda loud."

"Loud is good. Tell her to bring her lungs."

Well, lung power was not an issue for his sister, Yoli. Black women are internationally renowned for their bodacious buttocks, but Yoli was an example of the Pam Grier-Halle Berry tribe of big beauties. About five foot nine or so with a small waist and pretty face (though ironically not as beautiful as her brother's), this twenty-two-year-old was stacked like thousand-dollar chips at a poker table. And she knew it. The halter-style top she wore made it difficult to do anything but watch Yoli undulate. Yoli was such a sight I worried none of the A&R guys, traditionally a very horny crew, would even look at Brian onstage. Yoli's two pals, Patti and Delores, were both classic round-hipped black girls from Harlem—good looking, but not in Yoli's class.

"My brother's told me how you've helped him and I just wanted to say how grateful I am." I really tried to look directly into Yoli's small, dark brown eyes but it was so damn hard. Yoli knew her effect and giggled. "Should I have dressed more conservatively?"

"Hell no." She smiled at my response. "Let God's bounty be known."

"I know that's right," she replied and then gave me a deep hug that pushed her breasts against my chest. Blood started rushing around my body in all sorts of good directions. "After the show we'll all get something to eat together, won't we?" she asked. Of course I agreed, knowing full well I would be spending that time measuring the enthusiasm of the collected A&R execs.

Still, that hug put the idea I could fuck Brian's sister in my head (both of them). Her enthusiasm for me was to be expected. There were so few successful male figures in the black community that a man like me—a jive-ass showbiz Negro with lots of game and some slick conversation, who could handle himself in the white world as well as the black—could seem like Dr. King to a ghetto girl. This was especially true since her big brother respected me and I was about to bring heavy cheddar to the family dinner table. From her point of view, why not give Mr. Dark some? I mean, she was gonna fuck someone. I was safer than the local dope man and way flyer than any gainfully employed city bureaucrat.

But from my point of view, this was actually an absolutely terrible idea. Talk about complicating a relationship. Sleeping with a client's sister was always a bad idea, 'cause unless you planned on marrying her it could only end badly (and so could marriage, as well). So there was zero percentage in even contemplating slapping thighs with her.

I banished all this from my mind as Brian took the small stage in the SIR studio. Tailored in scarlet leather pants and jacket and an ebony silk shirt and boots, Brian looked as slick now as any current love man with a major label contract. I just crossed my fingers and took a deep breath. Would these A&R dudes sitting in judgment "get" him and see his potential? I'd heard Herman, the thin, elegant rep from Capitol, was in the closet, so I was optimistic that he'd fall in love with Brian. The brother from Def Jam was a hip-hop head who would quote Chuck D. over lunch, so I wasn't sure he'd get Brian or why he was even here. I also had representatives from RCA, Warner Bros., and Sony in the house.

I'd hired a crew of crack studio musicians to back my man. People like drummer Trevor Gale and guitarist Cornell Dupre, top-of-the-line, triple-scale players who, based on the rehearsals, made Brian elevate his game. Now, in the moment of truth, Brian sang strong and lean, confident in the knowledge that anywhere he went during his four-song set these brothers wouldn't simply follow him, but would enhance that journey.

I did get a sweet break. The Sony A&R man, a lanky, long-faced brother named Ted, had invited backup. Frances Hagan was a perky strawberry blonde who had made her rep in hip-hop, but was an old school soul girl at heart. We'd slow danced one night to a Dells record at her apartment and kissed but, for whatever reason, never went much further. But I knew she liked me. I hadn't invited her because Ted was much higher up on the food chain at Sony, but now that she was here, I knew she'd help me (as long as it didn't mean sticking her neck out too far).

Yoli and her two friends did their part. We'd worked on a Marvin Gaye medley that weaved "Distant Lover" with "After the Dance." From the first notes of "Distant Lover," the three swooned and yelled as Brian hit particularly sensual notes. The A&R guy from Warner Bros. cut me a look that said, "This is so unprofessional." All I could do is shrug. I didn't tell them when or how to act. I mean, it wasn't like I planned it this way. Their excitement wasn't an act, though it was somewhat premeditated.

By the time Brian got into the "After the Dance" part of the medley, Yoli, Patti, and Delores had jumped on the low stage and were grinding up against Brian and one another. The wildest thing was how Yoli got up against her brother and began rubbing her ample bosom up and down his body in a slow, highly incestuous jiggle. Clearly the Barneses were an open minded family.

After the set the Warner Bros. rep left without a word—apparently offended by the onstage action—while the Def Jam man was pleasant before exiting. Happily the reps from Sony, Capitol, and RCA lingered around, meeting Brian and chatting with me. No one wanted to show their hand around the others, but their presence said enough: they were all interested. When Ted and Frances offered to take us out to dinner I accepted. My man from Capitol was visibly pissed he hadn't spoken first. He did request a lunch with me the next day and I was quite happy to schedule that appointment.

The Sony duo took us to Jezebel, a black-owned restaurant in the theater district that featured New Orleans–style cuisine and the ornate decor of a French Quarter bordello. Subdued, rosy lighting, antique vases and lamps, lace table settings, and strategically placed plants set the mood. On the wall were Warhols of Muhammad Ali and Miriam Makeba. In the main dining room several white bench swings were suspended from the ceiling so you could savor your she-crab soup while lightly swaying.

In one of those swinging benches the three girls chatted and sipped drinks, while Ted, Frances, Brian, and myself sat in regular chairs and talked business. The Sony duo had heard the demo and had been impressed enough to come down. They wanted to know about Brian's influences, what kind of songs he liked, etc. It was a classy getting-to-know-you session and Brian handled himself well. I could tell Frances was smitten. She was tossing her hair a little more than necessary. Cool with me; a good A&R person has to fall a bit in love with his or her signee to do the job with passion.

While I was conducting business and guiding the

conversation, I was also ignoring the presence of a stocking-clad foot rubbing up my ankle and to my thigh. I suspected it was Yoli, but it could have been either of the other ladies on the bench. I slid my body over to minimize contact. I was in get-money mode. Flirting could wait.

At the end of the meal I made an appointment to come over to their office in two days—Ted and Frances had to run some numbers and talk to the higher-ups. I was expecting a substantial offer and told them so, and I also mentioned my scheduled lunch with Capitol the next day. After the shaking of hands, etc., I was beat. I always felt drained after a showcase and the politics that followed, but the Barnes clan wouldn't let me go.

So, against my better judgment, I ended up at Sweet-water's, a club/restaurant on Amsterdam Avenue in the Sixties that catered to a black suit-and-tie crowd. Yoli, Brian, and their two friends toasted me with bad champagne and then considered the possibilities: moving their mother from Harlem to a house in Jersey; new cars for everyone; one day headlining a show at the Garden. It was all doable, I told them, and they toasted me again.

By now I was getting a little tipsy. Yoli's toes were moving higher up my inner thigh. When Brian recognized some pals at the bar and walked over, I leaned over the table and asked Yoli, "What do you think you're doing?"

"I'm being friendly? What's wrong with that?

"Yeah," her friend Delores cut in. "What? You too good for Yoli?"

"No, ladies. I'm not too good for anyone. In fact, I'm not good at all. I'm a scandalous motherfucker through and through." On one level I said this to scare Yoli away. But, in truth, there's no better way to get a black girl wet than announce that you are a worthless motherfucker. Don't ask me why. I'm not a sociologist, I just know shit. Then I added, "But I don't mess with my money and *you* shouldn't mess with your brother's money."

"Damn," Yoli replied, "you too serious. I'm just being playful. You remind me of Benita."

"Brian's girlfriend. Too serious, huh?"

"Yeah. Just like you."

"Well, I know I'm not like Benita. I'm gonna make your brother some money. And I don't think Benita can do that."

"I hear that!" Patti chimed in. Yoli nodded and then high-fived me. The revelation that Yoli was unhappy with Benita was music to my ears. I needed Yoli whispering in her brother's ear, subverting that relationship and getting him ready for the road.

"Listen," I said to her, putting my mack on. "I think you are one beautiful, deeply sexy woman. Under other circumstances I'd be all over you. Tell you the truth, I'm feeling stupid right now 'cause I'm not trying to get with you."

Yoli's girlfriends eyed me curiously. Patti said, "My

goodness," and Delores shook her head slightly, like she peeped the suddenly manipulative change in my game. Yoli seemed pleased by my words. Even better, she blushed when she felt my shoeless foot rubbing up against the inside of her thigh. Seeing how open she was, I took my foot and slid the whole damn thing up her dress and between her legs, caressing her pussy with my big toe. Yoli took a big gulp of her champagne, then squeezed her thighs around my foot. I could feel a spot of wetness on the tip of my big toe.

I felt eyes on the side of my face so I turned slightly to my right. There was a dark chocolate lady in a red Lycra Patrick Kelly dress who was sipping a piña colada as she watched me toe fuck Yoli. The two suit-and-tie brothers sitting with her were too deep in conversation other with each other to notice her wandering gaze. Our eyes met. She waved her index finger slightly from left to right, pulled her red lips off her straw, and mouthed the word "naughty."

The idea of being so closely observed made me push my toe harder and deeper into Yoli's pussy. She was so hot my toe was being warmed by her. Her breathing was slow. My dick got hard at the thought of pleasing these two women at one time. Suddenly Yoli, who'd been remarkably cool, said, "I need to go to the ladies' room."

"You are coming back, right?" I asked.

"Yeah, Dark, but it may take me a minute."

Patti offered to go with her but Yoli insisted she stay

and have another drink. I slid my foot back into my shoe as Yoli swayed toward the spiral staircase. As Yoli turned down the steps I saw her look my way and then crook her finger in a "come here" gesture before disappearing from sight.

I hesitated a moment, thought better of it, then said, "Fuck it" and stood up to follow her. Then Brian came back to the table with an ugly, talkative dude named Jesus, a high school buddy of his who was managing a rap group from Mount Vernon, the home of Heavy D. Against my will I got sucked into a record biz convo for about ten minutes before I could slip away. As I wound down the spiral staircase, I passed by the table of the woman in red, and she glanced down at me, her eyes twinkling. Up close she looked real good—thick, juicy lips, short black curly hair, and a flush, hungry look. She actually looked familiar, but that was probably wishful thinking.

Yoli wasn't in the hallway when I got down there. I quietly cracked open the ladies' room door, peered inside to see two women who were carefully redoing their makeup in a mirror, neither of whom was Yoli. I slipped into the men's room and walked over to the stalls. Sadly Yoli wasn't in there, either. I knew it was for the best, but I can't say I wasn't disappointed. I took a leak, washed my hands, and left the men's room.

Standing against the wall smoking a cigarette was the woman in the red Patrick Kelly dress. I walked over to her and said, "Enjoying your smoke?"

"Would you like one?"

"I don't indulge."

She chuckled. "It didn't look that way to me."

"You've been paying attention."

"So," she said after a puff, "you don't remember me?"

"No," I had to admit. "But I wish I did."

"No worries," she reassured me. "We met at an album release party. You asked me for my number, but the guy who brought me was standing right there. You didn't seem to care, but I'm not that kind of girl."

"And I'm not usually that kind of guy. I must not have thought much of your date."

"Must not," she said and took another puff. And then, "My name is Shelly." She stuck out her not-smoking hand. I took, I held it, and she didn't mind.

"Hello again, Shelly."

She chuckled again. "How's the toe?"

"It's a little cramped, but I can still walk."

She took her hand out of mine and reached into the red purse slung over shoulder, pulling out a business card. Shelly Brunson. A CPA and a business manager in a sexy red dress.

She told me, "I've been a fan of yours for a long time."

"I'll keep you in mind," I said and then pocketed the card.

"And watching you and that girl made my night."

"Glad I could be of service," I replied.

There was a long pause. She took a last drag and then dropped the cigarette to the floor. I crushed it with my toe. We looked at each other. I took her hand again and slowly moved her toward me until there was a dime's worth of distance between us.

"Shelly?" I said with a questioning inflection.

"Yes," she replied to my unspoken question.

I took her into the men's room. Fucking Yoli certainly wasn't going to happen—not tonight anyway—but there was no need for all that foreplay to go to waste.

We went into a stall and locked it behind us. She reached into her purse and pulled out a vial of coke. I wasn't actually a coke kinda guy—I'd seen too many of my pals from the eighties knocked on their ass by it to be a regular subscriber. Still, decadent moments like this were why coke existed. I took a one-and-one and so did she. We rubbed our noses and felt the crystalline rush.

While she unbuckled my pants, I raised her dress, pushed down her pantyhose, and pushed aside her cherry-colored panties and went in raw. I pushed Shelly's small brown butt against the wall. In the distance I could hear the drumbeat of "Billie Jean" from upstairs and I did my best to fuck her to that rhythm. I felt a sharp bone at the top of her vagina rub against my dick with a soft hardness. Shelly quivered. She was already there—at least she'd had a small one—and I'd only pumped a couple of times. Lucky girl. I kept pushing Shelly's small brown butt up against the wall.

I think someone came in and took a leak, but I didn't care—that's what coke-fueled sex is all about—you pump away like a crazy rabbit in a carrot patch. I was in the vicinity of a big orgasm when Shelly started biting my earlobe. Not a sweet nibble. It was like my ear was a ballpark hot dog. Coke makes you short-tempered. So I just pulled my dick out of her and began zipping up my pants.

"What's wrong?"

"I'm going to finish my drink."

"But you didn't pop, baby."

"I'm okay. I'm saving it for later." I was being curt, but at that moment I suddenly realized I'd just had unprotected coke sex in a men's room. This would be high on the list of stupid moves for any man with money.

Now she was pissed. "Something wrong with my pussy?" she asked as she adjusted her red dress.

"No, Shelly. Not at all. I'm just tired."

"Shit," she said, "that's what the blow's for. What you got, a cramp in your dick now?"

"Yeah," I said, anxious to leave. "I have your business card. We'll be in contact."

"Yeah, we should do business," she said, realizing perhaps that I now might feel I owed her something. That brightened her mood and avoided a potentially embarrassing men's room argument.

When I got back to the table I found Yoli sipping on a piña colada. Her two friends had gone home to pay their baby-sitters. Brian had gone to meet Benita, who'd requested he pick her up at the hospital.

"Why'd you wait around?"

"It would be rude if you came back upstairs and no one was here."

"I was gone a long time."

"Yeah," she said with a bit of contempt. "A half hour. I went back down looking for you after we missed each other."

"Sorry about that."

"And," she continued, "I heard the moans of some bitch in heat coming from the men's room."

"Really?"

"Hell yeah. Yo, if that bitch looks at me like that again, it's her ass."

I glanced over my shoulder. Shelly, looking a little hazy and a touch hyper, was engaged in a staredown with Yoli. Her two male companions looked a little upset, too. I figured they were probably wondering a) where she's been?, b) what did she do?, c) what part did I play?, and d) who was this crazy big-breasted bitch aiming bedroom eyes at their companion? Judging this as a potentially explosive situation, I paid the tab and ushered Yoli out of Sweetwater's.

Outside on Amsterdam Avenue Yoli got loud with me. "You fucked that stank bitch in the men's room, didn't you? I can smell pussy on your body."

"Keep you voice down, Yoli," I ordered. Then in a

harsh whisper I added, "I'm a grown-ass man and I'll put my dick where I see fit. I cannot date you. I cannot kiss you. I cannot fuck you. That's it. End of discussion!"

She looked at me a moment with the face of a hurt five-year-old. Then she grabbed my head and kissed me hard and wet, like we were school kids making out in the back stairwell.

"Well," she said, pulling her head away, "you did kiss me. And it was good."

"Okay," I said. "Okay."

Yoli smiled, hugged me like a teddy bear, and then hailed a taxi uptown. Yoli would be my ally. Yoli would be a distraction. Yoli would not be my lover (I hoped).

I was waving down another cab when Shelly and her two companions walked past me down Amsterdam Avenue. She looked back at me and grabbed the ass cheeks of each suit-and-tie brother. All right, I thought. Hope those brothers are ready for a long night.

chapter 5
Turning Out B. Barnes

The night I turned out Brian Barnes we were a month into recording his Sony Records debut. We signed with them because they'd made a great offer and had only one new jack swing contender under contract (Johnny Kemp), and I was sure he'd be a one-hit wonder. Reason: zero sex appeal. Another benefit was that Frances had become our patron saint at the label, fighting successfully to give us more creative control than I'd expected.

I stood behind the producer and engineer as Brian crooned over a sharp, metallic drum program and a funky keyboard bass line. The contrast of the cold and hot of the rhythm track played well against Brian's vocal. We were almost ready.

Back in 1990 there were few giants on the R&B chart. Brian's chief competition was Al. B Sure!, who had a small voice at best, and Keith Sweat, who was a whiner. Luther Vandross, Freddie Jackson, etc., were older and sweeter with none of the youth appeal Brian had. Mr. Barnes could wail with desire, and the Sony people had paid us a pretty sum of money for it.

They were very excited about the Marvin Gaye medley as a way to attract both adult and urban radio programmers, plus fans would be comfortable with a familiar record. You gotta remember this was before every rap and R&B record sampled an eighties hit for its chorus or hook. Brian was actually a few years ahead of the game. Enough business talk—let's get back to sex.

I isolated Benita from Brian by keeping him in the studio and away from her house. I intercepted her calls to the studio. His vocal coaches advised against lengthy conversations with her (or anyone else, either) to rest his voice. He'd never sung this long or hard in his life so those vocal cords had to be protected, was the party line. He was working late nights and sleeping during the day, which was the exact opposite of her work schedule at Downstate.

Sure, much of the separation was instigated by me. However, it wasn't all part of my scheme. Brian, at his own behest, was being reconstructed from the ground up.

I had a cracked tooth in the back fixed and the yellowed fronts whitened. I had him grow a mustache that my barber carefully trimmed every three days. I hired a trainer to build up his chest for topless photo shoots and turn a soft belly into a six-pack or, at least, keep it flat and toned. I had a media trainer working on his gift for gab.

All these furious-paced activities had Brian focused on himself, upping his self-involvement and vanity, which aren't great qualities for maintaining a strong love relationship, but feed the ego a performer needs to win. I suspected, in truth, I was just expediting a process of disengagement Brian truly wanted. However, if I'd never shown up, I'm not sure he would have (or could have) done it on his own.

I took Brian to an East Side gourmet Chinese restaurant called Mr. Chow, where there would be a who's who clientele, including Upper East Side matrons, guys trying to impress their girls (and often their girl's family), and lots of music and media biz types. Black entertainment folks loved using it as an upscale Chinese takeout spot, so it was a place to be seen if you were in the record game. Part of my goal was to show off Brian to my peers.

And there was another part of the Mr. Chow clientele I was introducing Brian to on this night, who'd be arriving a bit after we did.

Mr. Chow had big mirrors on the far wall, so even if your back was to the front door you could still watch who came in and went out. Moreover, the dining area was sunken from street level, so everyone had to walk down steps to their table. This insured that everyone had to make an "entrance." I got us a table against the far wall and sat where I could look over Brian's shoulder and see the entrance in the reflection of the mirrored wall. We were having Mr. Chow's world famous squab and chicken saté when Brian's eyes lit up.

"Yo, man," he said in a loud whisper that didn't disguise his excitement. I gazed over his head and saw a willowy beauty in a short black dress speaking to the maître d'. The lady was half-black, half-Vietnamese, around five feet ten in her stocking feet (but tonight she was wearing three-inch heels), long, straight black hair, honey brown skin, the almond-shaped eyes of her mother, and the big, proud lower lip of her father. Protruding out of her clingy black dress was an ass that confirmed her African-American heritage.

"Damn, she's fine!" he said, stating the obvious.

"Yeah," I agreed. "Crazy exotic, huh? Her name's Mai Lei."

"You know her?"

"Sure," I said casually. "She's a stylist. Used to model. Wonder who she's meeting?"

Mai Lei walked over to the bar, which overlooked the dining room. When she crossed her legs and ordered a drink I though Brian would never breathe again.

"Who could have the balls to make that lady wait? They've got to be crazy," Brian observed.

"You know," I said, "maybe she'll join us. At least until her dinner companion gets here. What do you think, Brian? Perhaps she'd enjoy meeting you? She could become your stylist."

I had a deep hook in him now. It was all he could do not to leap out of his seat. "Yeah," he said anxiously. "I'm sure we could work together."

"Thought so." I smiled. "Let me go get her."

By the time I'd moved through the tightly packed tables, walked up the stairs, and arrived at the bar, Mai Lei had turned down two free drinks, an invitation to dine with a Wall Street tycoon (though she had taken his business card), and a weekend trip to the Cayman Islands. Actually she hadn't yet turned down the trip—she just hadn't said yes.

"Well," she said after I'd kissed her cheek, "is your singer gonna amuse me, Dark?"

"He's a red-blooded young black man. You know about that type, I believe."

"Is he gonna be a star?"

"I'll do my best."

"As I recall you are a very hard worker." She squeezed my arm.

"Flattery will get you lots of places, Mai, but then you know that. It's time for you to shake your head no."

"Yes," she said, even as her head made the universal gesture for no.

"Sorry, bro," I said to Brian when I returned to our table. "Looks like she's gonna wait at the bar."

"Who's she waiting on?"

"Oh, I didn't ask." Then I slid into a conversation about the tour I was lining up for him. This engaged Brian, but his eyes darted up toward Mai Lei every couple of minutes. He had to know who the lucky man was who got to eat with her. About twenty minutes later Brian interrupted me. "Yo, yo, look who's coming."

I looked up at the mirror over Brian's head and saw Mai Lei move through the chairs toward us—just like we'd arranged. "I think I'm being stood up," she announced when she arrived at our table.

"That's terrible," I said, and then introduced her to Brian. "Please join us. Is that all right with you, Brian?"

"Oh, sure."

I sat Mai Lei next to Brian and watched him leer at her, his mind clouded by his proximity to her beauty, his loins enthralled by her lips. After a few moments of small talk I continued the education of Brian Barnes. "I got those tickets for you, Mai."

"Front row for Luther Vandross at Radio City?"

"That's right."

She leaned her long body across Mr. Chow's white tablecloth and pressed her lips against mine. A short, moist meeting of our mouths that made Brian's eyes widen.

"Dark," she said, "you kept your promise."

"For you, always."

"Would you like to walk me to the ladies' room?"

"Sure," I replied. "Brian, could you help me move this table back so Mai can slide out?" Brian did as he was told but otherwise was silent. "Be a minute."

Again he nodded. He watched with big baby eyes as Mai and I moved through the tables and chairs. My left hand briefly cupped her ass as we walked up the steps, past the maître d', and into the men's room. We came out fifteen minutes or so later, looking both flushed and guilty. Brian was eating green tea ice cream, his eyes locked on us like a hunter on a deer. Before we went back to the table I had one more card to play.

Sitting at the bar was a busty, redbone, freckle-faced Creole lady with a low-cut dress and a high-post attitude. Brione waved at Mai, who walked over and gave her a tongue kiss that made every man (and a few of the women) quiver. I exchanged greetings with Brione, kissed Mai again, and then watched (along with everyone in Mr. Chow) as they exited the restaurant.

"What's up with that?" Brian wondered when I sat back down and sipped jasmine tea.

"Well," I said with faux modesty, "it looks like I'm gonna have to leave you. I hate being rude and all, but, well . . ." I paused.

"Well, *what,* Dark?"

"Look, I know you're in a committed relationship and I wouldn't wanna endanger that in any way."

By now Brian's curiosity had overwhelmed him. I had the brother's mind in the palm of my hand.

"C'mon, Dark, let a brother know what's going on."

"Well, Mai—you know the girl I just went in the men's room with?"

"Yeah, yeah," he said impatiently. "Of course I know who you're talking about."

"Well, she just blew me in the men's room because of those Luther Vandross tickets."

"You lying!"

"Keep your voice down," I said. "And, no, I'm not lying. Now she wants me to meet her at her apartment where I could fuck her and her friend."

"All that for Luther Vandross?"

"Hey, man, I guess they love that song 'Any Love.' But my point was I'm not gonna ask you to come with me. No way would I put you in a position like that. I'll have my driver take you home and I'll take a cab to her place."

Brian looked at me, his mouth open, his hand holding a spoonful of green tea ice cream. He was struggling to form words. I didn't help him. There were eighteen million questions racing through his cranium. The most important ones were: How do you do this and why can't I? Brian expressed both ideas with the question: "How often does this happen to you?"

"It's an occupational hazard of being in the music biz. Girls love the music. They love the parties. They love the stars. If you were already established they'd be asking you to join them. Shit, they might not even have asked me—tickets or no tickets. But you're not. You're just an unknown vocalist with a nurse girlfriend waiting on you. I might be able to convince them that you're going to be a star and tonight would be, you know, an investment in the future."

"Yeah," he said excitedly. "That's true."

"But I can't make you single. I can't make you free to savor all the pussy that's headed your way. I'm only your manager."

Fifteen minutes later we stood on East Fifty-seventh street in front of Mr. Chow with my driver holding the Towncar door open for Brian. Brian killed time, asking me questions about his record's release and the timing of his all important tour. Of course all he really wanted was to come with me to wherever those two beautiful girls were waiting.

I acted determined not to tempt him. I wasn't going on record telling him, "Come with me to fuck these women." No, I wanted Brian to invite himself into this world with me.

Which is why I said, "Brian, I gotta go. You have my number. If you need me, call me anytime." Brian shook my hand and took off. I hailed a cab and headed down Second Avenue toward Murray Hill in the east thirties, a section of town full of unreasonably priced apartments where groups of single women resided in large numbers. Some were trust fund babies. Some were models. A few were escorts who used looks and charm to feed Manhattan's hungry businessmen.

My taxi was in the mid-thirties when my cellphone rang. A smile stretched across my face. "Okay," I said in reply. "I do understand."

As I waited under the awning at Mai Lei's building on East Thirty-second Street, I smoked a Macanudo cigar. After tonight Brian would view me differently. More importantly Brian would never see himself the same again. The Towncar rolled up and Brian didn't wait for the driver to open the door before he was out on the sidewalk.

"Listen, Brian," I said as he stood before me, his breathing as labored as a Little Leaguer before his first at bat. "Before we go upstairs I just wanna tell you something."

"Sure," he replied, irritated by the delay in this unexpected and, hopefully, not to be regretted experience.

I told him, "I am your manager. That means I make things happen for you. Especially things you didn't even know you wanted."

"I hear you, Dark."

"And I keep secrets. From now on your secrets are also mine. Do you understand?"

"Yes, I do."

"Good. Well, don't you think the ladies have waited long enough?"

Marvin Gaye's "I Want You" tickled our ears and the

smell of sandalwood incense teased our noses as we walked through the door of penthouse number one. The room was inviting, yet anonymous. The sleek, modern furnishings were bathed in a rosy light designed to soothe senses. No family pictures. No school diplomas. The only art on the walls were blurry photos of body parts in intimate motion. Neither Mai Lei nor Brione were in sight, but their dresses, underwear, and shoes lay strewn in the center of the living-room floor.

Brian was about to speak, but I put my index finger to my mouth to silence him and then a hand to my ear, urging him to listen. Below the throbbing bass line and Marvin's melodious voice were other sounds, female sounds, from a hallway off the living room. I crooked my finger for Brian to follow and them moved quietly down the hall and into the darkness. The scent of sandalwood grew more pungent with each step forward.

From under a bedroom door there was a scarlet glow. I put my ear to the door and motioned for Brian to join me. Together, like two naughty boys trying to hear grown-ups do "da nasty," we pressed our ears against the door and heard low, steady moans.

"Damn," Brian whispered and then giggled. Suddenly the door flew open and Brian and I stumbled into the room like clowns.

"Good evening, gentlemen," said Mai, who lay on a king-size bed with her long legs spread wide open and her hairless pussy lips moist and pouty.

"How are you, Mai?" I said.

"Fine. I see you brought company," she said and nodded toward my young companion. He was about to say something when a pair of pale, freckled hands came from behind him and grabbed his groin.

"Oh," Brione said into his ear, "I don't mind that he's here. Just as long as he does what he's told." Her tongue flicked into his ear and Brian moaned. I believe he came a little bit right there. But that was just foreplay. Mai rose from the bed and pressed her naked body against his. Brione kissed him about the neck and face. Together the ladies began undressing him. His clothes seemed to evaporate from his body and with their liquidation went his inhibitions.

Mai placed a condom on his dick using her mouth and then turned around, offering Brian her ample ass. He entered her harshly, like he was afraid she'd change her mind. Brione was the wild card, placing her hands between his buttocks and sliding her small red tongue between them. With that new element Brian's legs nearly buckled and his rhythm with Mai changed. He went from a rigid, military beat to a herky-jerky motion. Brione took Brian's balls with her left hand and continued to explore his ass with her tongue.

This combination of intercourse and anal pleasure was all new to my man and he made sounds from deep in his throat like an animal. Then his sounds grew musical, like the ad-lib at the end of a song. It was a sound I'd heard from him often in the studio; it was a sound of freedom and sensuality. It was the sound that would make hits. It was the sound that would one day be the sound track for thousands of sexual acts by lovers all over this country and all over this world. Brian hit a high note as he filled the condom and his lean body shook.

As the ladies guided Brian to the bed, I scooped up the used condom in a tissue and walked out of the room. I liked Mai—she was real good at her job—but I couldn't trust her with potentially multimillion-dollar sperm.

I flushed the condom down the toilet and then glanced at myself in the mirror. Was I a businessman solidifying a relationship with a client or some kind of pimp stealing the virtue of a young man for sport? The truth lay somewhere in between.

I stuck my head into the bedroom and watched as Mai Lei and Brione ministered to Brian's body with their lips and tongues. Mai kissed his forehead, his cheeks, and his chest with little sweet pecks. Brione sucked his toes, first one at a time and then taking two and three into her mouth at a time. Then the two beauties moved slowly toward Brian's groin from both ends of his prone body.

Even before they'd reached his dick it was flush with blood, revived by the kind of expert foreplay a man only experiences a few times in his life. I've always thought that once a man's been with a truly gifted and sexually mature woman it's damn hard to truly yearn for a virgin or some other sexually inexperienced lover. Only from the experience of true ecstasy can you understand what your body is capable of, that's what my years on the road had taught me. Now Brian was learning that same lesson. After Mai slipped on a condom, she worked her hand over his shaft and teased his tip with her tongue, while Brione sucked his nuts and leaned down to tickle the area between his balls and ass.

I know I sound like an old voyeur, but I was truly enjoying Mai and Brione's efforts. This wasn't some go-for-yours, trooper orgy. This was an event intricately choreographed by me and I was savoring my stage craft. When Brian came again, gushing into the condom until it popped up and then sagged, I almost let out a cheer. Both ladies turned to look my way and I gave them the thumbs-up sign. As I turned away I could hear Brian starting to snore.

I was in the living room sipping cranberry and vodka, and puffing my Macanudo cigar, when Mai, dressed in a Japanese kimono, came in and sat next to me. Her lips were puffy and plump. I wanted to suck them like lollipops.

"He's asleep," she announced and then took the drink out of my hand and helped herself to a taste.

"What do you think?" I asked.

"I like him. He's got a few hygiene problems, though. You need to get him some new cologne and he badly needs a pedicure." I assured her that I'd get all that fixed tomorrow. "So," she asked, "all you're doing tonight is watching?"

"Aren't you tired?"

"Come on, Dark. I really didn't do that much."

"Is that right? Well, all I want is for you to kiss me with those amazing lips."

"You know," she replied with mock seriousness, "more sexually transmitted diseases are passed via the mouth than any other orifice."

"Well, that's all I want from you. Just for me to stick my tongue way up inside that mouth of yours and taste vodka and cranberry and whatever else you got up there."

"You trying to get real personal there, Mr. Dark."

"That's the only kind of sex I need tonight, Mai, so don't front. Just give me what I want."

I took her by her shiny black hair and pulled Mai toward me, pressing my black man lips against her black and Vietnamese lips, feeling the cushy texture against mine and slowly biting her lips and then traveling that silken road into her mouth.

She pulled away and looked me in the eye. "What are you doing to me, Dark?"

"I got no words," was my reply. I took her lips and mouth in mine and, like two teenagers in a wood-paneled suburban basement, Mai and I just kissed and kissed.

chapter 6
Ma's Party

The album release party for Brian's self-titled debut was a glitzy affair at Club 20/20, a restaurant/nightclub in the Flatiron District that was fronted by Nickolas Ashford and Valerie Simpson, two great songwriter-performers who'd penned several of Marvin Gaye's duets with Tammi Terrell. (Today, the location houses an upscale strip club.) It also had been the site of Keith Sweat's *Make It Last Forever* album release party a few years before, so I was hoping all these historical R&B connections would be good omens for us.

I'd made sure the crowd balanced slick R&B stars (Freddie Jackson, Kashif) with new jack energy (members of Guy and Today, Heavy D) 'cause I saw Brian as a bridge between the past and the future. I'd also reached out to an ad hoc group called the Black Girls Coalition, a charity organization of most of the city's top models. So lovelies like the classy Gail O'Neal, the drop dead gorgeous Karen Alexander, the elegant Akure Wall, and the regal Veronica Webb were in the house. It was Brian's first contact with these slender, sophisticated sisters and he was definitely a little intimidated when I ushered a couple of them over to his table.

The person who was really irritated by their presence was his now ex-girlfriend Benita, who I'd invited but had exiled to a corner table where she and two girlfriends stared daggers at the models floating around Brian. Though they had yet to have a formal break-up it was clear to anyone with eyes that Brian's days of monogamy were long gone.

However, the featured event of the night was meeting Brian's mother. He'd kinda kept her in the background during the recording process—I'd spoken to her on the phone a couple times to send her money or gifts—but somehow we'd never met. The night of the album release party I learned why. Mrs. Barnes didn't just give birth to Brian—she'd spit him out. Much more so than her daughter, Brian's face was a bigger, rounder version of hers. His handsomeness was her beauty.

But where Brian seemed an innocent soul interested in being corrupted, Jezebelle Barnes had clearly been around the barn so often she knew all the chicken(heads). There was a slutty, dress-too-tight quality to Mrs. Barnes (Brian's father being the first of three husbands) that made her a sight to behold in her rabbit coat, beige leather skirt and shoes, sheer black blouse, and dangling gold-plated earrings. She'd brought along a slightly demure but still-ghetto best friend, Esther, along with Yoli, in the limo her son had provided. Her first words to me after we were introduced were, "There sure are some fine looking men in here tonight," and her second set of words were, "I don't want any champagne but a Bacardi and coke would be nice."

Bacardi it was for Mamma Barnes. Though she now toiled as a manager of a bar in Washington Heights, Jezebelle had once been an R&B singer herself, working first in a girl group, the Queenettes, and later cutting two singles on a small New York label before getting pregnant and hanging up the microphone. Yoli had shown no musical talent so Jezebelle had doted on Brian, pushing him into talent shows, voice lessons, and so on. She'd started the vocal group he'd recorded with as a vehicle for Brian. When it failed, Jezebelle took it hard, hitting the bottle and losing control of her son. Benita, apparently, had filled his mother's place in his life.

And now I had. I was his new anchor and, according to his mother, it was the first time he'd had a male role model.

"That boy really respects you," she said to me at one point and sipped on her Bacardi. "He ain't really had a father." I was hoping she would say more. Maybe drop a gem of insight or two on me. But I got nothing else worthwhile 'cause right then, looking lean and languid, his long black hair looking fabulous on his shoulders, Nick Ashford came walking by.

"Oh," Jezebelle exclaimed, "you so fine."

The next thing anyone knew she'd leaped out of her seat and locked her arms around Ashford's skinny frame.

"This is Brian Barnes's mother," I said sheepishly, lest the veteran songwriter get offended. Ashford handled it well. He smiled stiffly as he peeled her off him and then quickly headed into the restaurant's kitchen area.

Brian saw what happened and came over to his mother and began speaking to her in a harsh whisper. He was scolding her like she was a naughty girl and he was Daddy. Watching them I got the feeling this was something they both were used to. I moved away after a while, sensing this moment was too personal to drop in on.

The rest of the evening was uneventful. Yoli squeezed my butt at one point. I just smiled and kept on moving. Wasn't messing with any more of these extreme Barnes women tonight.

As the party waned I found Brian talking with two Sony executives by the bar. He held a Coke in his hand.

He was nodding as they talked of his upcoming promotional tour. I was gonna go over and save him. A couple of model friends were wondering where we were going next. But it felt like this wasn't the night to push my star. It was a night for girls to watch him from a distance. His mother had been woman enough.

chapter 7
Doing Da Butt

After his introduction to the world of rhythm & pussy, Brian now saw me as his guide and confessor. Empowered by his record deal, the advance money, and the confidence that his career really getting started brought, Brian became a name dropper, but the name he was dropping was his own. At clubs around the city he'd let ladies know he had a record deal and would soon be a star. Very often he got the brush off. Occasionally he got a phone number. After all, he was still raw when he came to the art of using celebrity to seduce.

But at this early stage, sometimes he'd get lucky. And when he did, Brian would call me, quite excited, wanting to share the experience and show me that he was learning his lessons well. These pre-dawn debriefings became a feature of our relationship. I remember the first call like it was yesterday.

"Hello?" I said, quite groggy. It was around 3:30 A.M.

"Hey man, it's Brian. Can I tell you something?" Brian sounded strange. Tired, but with a weird urgency in his voice.

"Any time. You know that. What's up?"

"I fucked this girl in her ass tonight, man."

"Ohhh. And did you like it?"

"I did, but, well, you know, I got a question."

"Okay. What is it?"

"That doesn't make me gay, does it?"

"No. No way."

"Okay, that's good. You know it was her idea I do it."

"Well, there you go. You weren't looking for it. You didn't ask for it. It was offered and you partook. Tell me all about it."

"Well, I went down to Nell's on 14th Street with a buddy of mine and a spotted this fine-ass Latin girl drinking with her girlfriend at the bar. Turned out she was Dominican. Named Suzie Salgado. Nice light brown girl with the shiny hair she had pulled back in a bun. Nice eyes. Full lips that kinda made a circle when she looked at you."

"Like insert here, huh?"

"Exactly."

"Brian, you tell her you were a singer?"

"Yeah. But at first she didn't believe me. She made me sing into her ear to prove it. I could tell that got her excited."

"That's how you do it, my man."

"But the thing that got me hot was her backside."

"Dominican girls have an amazing ass-to-hip ratio."

"What?"

"Ass-to-hip ratio. A small waist makes a real round butt look enormous."

"Damn, it was like you were there, Dark. Tiny waist and hips that came out on either side like two balloons."

"So what did you do next? You got me up now, so I want details."

"I rapped to her a bit, you know. She was a physical therapist for old people. She started rubbing my shoulder and had a strong-ass grip. Told me she knew about every muscle group in the body. So I said let's see how you move your muscle groups. I was trying to be smooth, Dark."

"I see."

"So we went downstairs to that little dance floor. Dark, we weren't out there a minute when she turned around and put that butt up against my dick. It felt so good I almost busted right then."

"Big and soft, huh?"

"And hard, too."

"Word?"

"Dark, man, she could control her cheeks so they could feel soft and then she'd clench some muscles in her ass and she could kinda grip my dick up in her crack."

I just busted out laughing. Brian had run into one of the greatest ass freaks of all time but it was his amazement that made it funny.

"So you took her right home after that, huh?"

"No, Dark, it wasn't that easy. Her girlfriend was cock blocking. She just stood near the side of the wall sipping on a drink with a stank attitude, like she was jealous she wasn't getting no play. I just knew she wouldn't let Suzie leave alone."

"I hate that shit. Just 'cause your friend is having fun, don't stop the flow."

"Hell yeah."

"But something good happened."

"Yeah, two girls they knew came over. I was lucky 'cause they apparently didn't like Suzie—too much butt for them I guess. They were going to hit another club but now Suzie had me and her girlfriend had them, you know."

"Lucky man."

But also, Dark, it's like you say: this singing shit is like Spanish Fly. Suzie might have just given me her telephone number that night. You know, got me so open so I'd call her but not given up no ass, if I hadn't went over to the DJ booth and pulled out my demo of 'After the Dance.' "

"That material is not mixed, Brian."

"I know, Dark, but it was cool, man. I went over to that Sade-looking DJ Belinda."

"Yeah, she's got an amazing ass herself."

"Yo, if I hadn't been all over Suzie I would have stepped to her."

"Believe me, many have tried."

"So Belinda lets Suzie listen to my track through the earphones and then drops the song up in her mix right behind Guy's 'I like.' Belinda told me the only other person she does that for is Prince."

"How did the crowd react?"

"Great. She cut it with 'Sexual Healing' and the crowd went mad. After that Suzie was all in."

"That's all beautiful, Brian. You already made my morning. So let's get to the ass fucking part."

"Okay. Suzie lives out in West New York, just over the river from the city in one of those towers. Drove over in her Volkswagen rabbit."

"You took your life in your hands for that ass, Brian."

"I didn't mind. She kept calling me the next Michael Jackson so I didn't mind that car. Her crib was small but very nice. Very clean. A one bedroom with a view of the city. But here's the bugged part—she had all those pictures of women's butts on the wall."

"A bootiologist, huh?"

"I guess so. These were these three beautifully

framed photos of ass cheeks. Black and white. Very artsy looking. Turned out they were all of her butt, Dark."

"I see where this is going."

"Yeah. So I asked her about the photos. Suzie says, 'Since I was a little girl people have always made a big deal about my butt. Girls used to call me 'roast beef.' Even when I was just ten and eleven men would comment on it in the street. I used to be ashamed of it, but eventually I learned that there was power in my booty.'"

"That's a wise young woman right there, Brian."

"So after that I just put my hands all over that ass. It shook and moved like nothing I've ever felt before. Then Suzie said, 'Put your face between my cheeks.'"

"Her pants are still on at this point?"

"Yeah."

"Damn."

"So then she pulls her pants down and she's got nothing on, no panties, no underwear."

"Buck naked."

"Buck buck naked. And check this out—the ass smelt like perfume."

"There's not an ass made by God that smells like perfume."

"Well, this butt must have been made 'cause it smelled like Chanel No. 5 or something like that. So now I'm kissing her cheeks and she says, 'Stick your finger in my pussy.' So I do and she starts moaning, real deep moaning. Then Suzie says, 'Lick my asshole.' "

"Damn. I need this woman's number."

"I'm not too sure about this, Dark. It is still her shit hole, you know. But before I can say that she's kinda pushed her ass back and her cheeks opened and her asshole came towards me like an eyeball opening."

"This Suzie brought out the poet in you."

"I don't know if that's true, Dark, but what I did next did surprise me. I puckered up and that asshole puckered up and we kissed. Felt like if that ass had a tongue it would have Frenched me."

I just laughed at that. Nothing to say to something as crazy as that except, "What happened next?"

"Well, she shook when I did that and my finger got drenched. She took me by the free hand and, while I continued fingering her, she took me into her bedroom. Suzie guided me to the bed, sat me down, and then moved into the bathroom."

"And came out with KY Jelly?"

'How'd you know that?'

"That's how it's done, Brian."

"I put my jimmy on and grabed her around the waist. I got in there doggy style and, man, I almost nutted right then, the stuff was so good. Then Suzie flipped it on me—"

"She told you to stick it in her ass?"

"She didn't say anything. It's what she did."

"Go on."

"Now I'm riding her, right? While I'm doing that she pulled out that KY Jelly and squirted it all up into her asshole. At this point I just kinda stopped and looked at what she was doing. Next thing I know she's got one of her fingers up her ass, poking and digging up there."

"Did you now get the hint?"

"Well, not yet. I just started pumping again 'cause she was already moaning and grunting like nothing I'd ever heard before."

"So when did you do the deed?"

"Well, Dark it was like this: she reached back, grabbed my dick out of her pussy, and shoved it up in her ass."

Now I was rolling. I dropped the phone. I doubled over. This was too damn funny.

"What are you laughing at?"

"I didn't know, Brian."

"Didn't know what?"

"That you could make shit up like this. You had me. You really did."

"Dark, I didn't make up a damn thing. This happened. Just three hours ago."

"You expect me to believe she just popped your dick in like a lollypop?"

"Like it was natural as breathing."

"You are lying."

"I'm telling you every word is true. And I'm also telling you it freaked me the fuck out."

"Okay. I'm gonna say I believe you for a second. Let me ask you the million-dollar question."

Brian, who'd been running his mouth almost non-stop for a half hour, got quiet. "Oh man," he said finally. "It was so intense, it was so strange. I busted but the whole time I felt—I don't know. I felt I was doing wrong."

"Would you do it again?"

"Maybe."

"Maybe. Well, this isn't the last time you'll be offered a chance to do stuff like this. This is your life from now on. Lots of decisions, my man. Lots." Brian didn't say anything—just kind of sighed. "And you know what really scares you."

"What? You a mind reader now?"

"What scared you was that you enjoyed it. You went outside your experience. You saw something freaky in yourself and you're not sure it's a good thing."

"It was a trip. It felt good but it didn't feel good. I feel real fucking conflicted. I've never felt my body and mind at war like that before."

"Here's what's really scary. At a certain point you won't be conflicted. You'll just go with it. That's when you'll do anything and not worry about what it says about you. You'll just go for it."

"Here's what's funny, Dark: Suzie said the same thing. She said I'd get used to it."

"You gonna see her again?"

"I think so. I mean, she has a nice personality."

"A nice personality? Okay Brian, I gotta go back to sleep."

"You got any closing words of wisdom?"

"Wash your damn dick. And use detergent. See you in the A.M."

chapter 8
Sister Love in Philly

Philly had once been the epicenter of R&B. From the
days of Chubby Checker's
"The Twist" through the days of the Spinners and
O'Jays, right up to "Ain't No Stoppin' Us Now," the
Philly sound had set trends and made stars. However,
by 1990 the flood had slowed to a trickle and only
Boyz II Men were maintaining the city's legacy of
chart-topping R&B.

But while the hits had slowed, the city's appetite for
good music was still apparent. If you were doing R&B,
jazz, classical, or hip-hop, you still had to gain Philly's
love to be considered a major act. At this point Brian
Barnes was a baby act whose recently released single was

still percolating under the R&B radar. So we were playing Philly to generate goodwill in this crucial market.

A prominent local radio DJ did a weekly gig spinning at Zanzibar Blue, a Center City hot spot that attracted a lot of the local music community. If we did him a solid it might help get the Marvin Gaye medley, "Distant Lover/After the Dance," our first single, in rotation and some buzz in town. It should have been a track date (you sing over prerecorded music) to save money, but I wanted Brian Barnes taken seriously, so I forked over the money to bring a full band down from New York. Our official tour would begin in D.C., but this was a good chance to test out Brian and the band while helping his just-launched single. Besides, we could hop a late train and be in our own beds by 1:00 A.M.

Of course, we didn't have to go home. In my experience Philly women who loved music came in two types: earthy, gritty chicks who had no problem getting busy if you sang the right melody, and dreamy romantics for whom sex is a sacrament and intercourse an incense-supported blessing. Not as edgy as New York ladies, not as friendly as Atlanta peaches, or as fine as L.A. starlets, Philly women have their own vibe, one that could be quite accommodating to music men.

We checked into rooms at a Center City Marriott (just in case we wanted to stay the night), grabbed some hoagies (Brian's first), and then rolled over to the venue for the soundcheck. A couple of cute waitresses were setting up for the night. As the band warmed up I checked out the *Philadelphia Inquirer* and saw in the sports section that the Penn Relays were starting the next day at Franklin Field.

Though not explicitly a "black" event, most of the athletes would be brothers and sisters. A lightbulb went off in my head. I borrowed the manager's office phone and his Philly phone book and began working. Five calls later and Brian Barnes had been booked to sing the national anthem before next day's event.

"A track meet?" Brian wondered. "Is that really a good gig?"

"It puts you in front of thousands of people who've never heard of you—many of them extremely physically fit young women. Believe me, it's worth spending a night in Philly for."

The Zanzibar Blue gig turned out to be surprisingly tasty. Luckily for us, that evening's party was being cosponsored by the local health care workers' union, which translated into plenty of hardy, hard-partying nurses. Brian, based on his relationship with Benita, was into nurses, so I saw this as a good omen.

When Brian's name was first announced the initial response was tepid. Most of the local angels of mercy were unfamiliar with him. To smooth that over I had Brian open with Teddy Pendergrass's "You Got What I Want," a real sexual wake-up call that made my man's artistic intentions clear. That got some of the hefty sisters in attendance to sway their proud hips.

Brian saw the response and asked, "Do you wanna hear some more Teddy?" The crowd shouted "yeah!" and Brian did an impromptu, mostly a capella rendition of "Turn Out the Lights," which produced cheers from Philly's hot mamas. By the time he introduced his Marvin Gaye–inspired single, the dance floor was full and vibing to his new jack swing take on "After the Dance." Sagely, like any pro, he'd reached out to a heavy-set sister with braids and brought her onstage, where he grinded his pelvis into her as he sang. Everybody loves to see a big sister getting love—the other heavy-set sisters do and so do the skinny-ass girls. Everybody thinks it's fun. I was amazed that Brian seemed, almost instinctively, to know that showbiz trick.

After the performance, we set up a table where Brian signed posters, gave out promotional cassette singles, and kissed a few cheeks. Two particularly lovely cheeks belonged to a lady who introduced herself as Skakiya Cummings, a dark brown lollypop with blonde, close-cropped hair, a sly smile, and a round bubble ass that demanded respect. Immediately I sensed that Skakiya was a type number one Philly female, which meant things could get hot real quick.

Brian was immediately, and rightly, smitten. He asked her to hang around and have dinner with us. Skakiya had just stopped in for a quick drink with her friends. "I'm actually on my way to work, darlin'," she told him.

"How you gonna save people," he joked, "if you go in there doing CPR high?"

"I only had one piña colada," she protested. "Besides, I'm a better nurse if I'm relaxed."

"I hear that," he replied, eyeing Skakiya like a cat eyes tuna.

"If you really wanna see me, you'll page me later. If it's not a busy night, who knows?"

After she'd left, Brian said, "Homegirl was real aggressive and shit."

I schooled him, saying, "She's thirty plus, has a dope body, and no wedding ring. What's she got to be shy about? If she wants to fuck your singing self, she will."

"You think she's too long for me, Dark?"

"Old? Women really don't even know how to fuck until they're at least twenty-eight. That nurse will fire you up. Believe that."

"Yo, you know I love nurses."

"Yes, I do."

I'd turned in for the night when I got a call around 1:30 in the morning. It was Brian. "Yo, man, I'm gonna run and see that nurse, but I don't know how to get to the hospital."

Which is how I ended up in a taxi at 2:00 A.M. with my horny young client heading to the hospital. I'd tried to talk him out of this nocturnal mission. Having failed at that, I knew it was better I went with Brian rather than let him venture out into a strange city by himself. I didn't see this being a full manifestation of the Fever. It felt more like some horny young boy shit.

We entered the hospital through the emergency room, which was a pretty depressing place on a Friday night in Philly. Battered women. Bullet wounds. Drug ODs. When Skakiya appeared, we were both quite relieved to get out of that space. We followed her up to the pediatric ward, which was blissfully quiet except for one little girl who twisted and turned a bit. Brenda, Skakiya's coworker, a middle-aged sista with a bad attitude, wasn't happy to see us and threatened to report this violation of policy to their supervisor.

"What if we could be useful?" I asked.

"Useful?" she snorted. "How you two pussy hounds gonna be useful?"

I sat Brian down by the restless little girl and had him softly sing a lullaby. At first it seemed a waste. But slowly her breathing slowed and the turning ceased. She even began snoring. This placated Brenda, who went back to the nurses' station with a promotional cassette, while Skakiya guided Brian to a private room to "talk."

I lingered in the hallway and found a chair near the room's door. I must have dozed off—fifteen, twenty minutes—when a knocking sound awakened me. It was strong and rhythmic, like a drum machine. I rose from my chair and peeked in the room. In my experience medical women—nurses, interns, med school students, full-on doctors—were some of the most passionate females I've ever encountered. I saw that Brian was learning that happy lesson.

Atop a big hospital bed, illuminated by the light from an elevated TV, Skakiya rode Brian with a vengeance, her green nurses smock pulled down around her large nipples and her pants askew. She used her red-nailed hands to brace herself against the bed's bars, pushing that amazing butt down on Brian's groin. My man was being beast fucked by the eager nurse. The banging sound was Brian's head tapping against the bed frame with each of Skakiya's thrusts. His shirt was open and his pants pulled down. I got the distinct impression that the nurse had thrown him down on the bed and just had her way with him.

I busted out laughing. In response the nurse turned, cut me an evil eye, and ordered, "Shut the damn door!" Then she went back to handling her business. Still chuckling, I closed the door and took my seat. The sun was up when I was awakened by a hard shake. It was the unfriendly face of Brenda: "Get your friend and yourself out of here before that crazy girl gets me fired!"

I stumbled into the private room and there was Brian Barnes, snoring loudly and still half-clothed, with Skakiya laying right next to him.

I'd seen some strange scenes in my life, but this was right up there. I pulled Brian out of the bed, waking him and his lover up. They kissed and then she ran down the hall to the ladies' room. Brian was so wrecked I almost wanted to cancel the Penn Relays gig, but singing on a few hours sleep is a way of life on the road. Let him learn early on, I thought.

The last person I saw sing the national anthem wearing shades was José Feliciano and that man was blind. The excuse we offered the organizers was a severe eye infection. Brian's eyes were red, but it wasn't from a disease. The big-bodied Skakiya had squeezed every ounce of juice out of my client's twenty-three-year-old body and left him so high and dry I was considering intravenous fluids.

The national anthem is challenging enough when a singer's at the top of his game. However, if he's barely awake it is a plain nightmare. So my guile in getting him this gig may have backfired, since he was hoarse and rather awkward in his delivery. Applause was polite at best, and a few old heads were definitely not feeling the shades.

After the performance all Barnes wanted to do was go back to New York and to his bed. As a good manager I should have taken him to the Thirtieth Street station and tucked him snuggly into a seat. Instead I stuffed some crisp twenties in his palm and handed him his ticket. I told him I was gonna meet with some local radio people and hailed him a cab.

I felt a little guilty, but then if he was gonna do late-night fucking and then try to perform, he had to feel the consequences. A day in this game is a lesson, but you have to be your own teacher.

Once Brian was safely off to Amtrak, I went back into Franklin Field and took a seat near the locker rooms, where I could ogle the beautiful brown posteriors of the female sprinters and relay runners. There is no more powerful example of classic Afrocentric architecture than the ass, legs, and thighs of the sisters living this athletic life. They may not have the most beautiful faces in our community and their hair may get messed up by their sweaty activities, but their bodies are sculpted by God into true black Amazons.

I bought some binoculars and settled back to watch the long-limbed black beauties dash, jump, and leap for my enjoyment. Sure, they came to win medals for themselves and their colleges but, as far as I was concerned, the Penn Relays existed for me to bask in the glory of well-toned black womanhood.

A woman lined up for the two-hundred-meter hurdles caught my eye. She had a long, proud face with a high forehead and dramatic cheekbones. Her eyes were dark brown ovals lined top and bottom with thick, curly eyelashes. Her lips were so pouty I thought they could block the sun from her chin. Her hair was slicked back, shiny and black. Probably five feet eight, with small breasts wrapped in a burgundy Temple University tank top, a tapered waist, and thighs that could crush an apple into sauce. When she walked her butt shook arrogantly, daring you to look away and knowing there's no way in hell you could. The program said her name was Tonique Mannly, born in Barbados and representing Temple.

I watched her stretch and prepare. When she got into the blocks for her event my heart pounded, both in rooting interest for Tonique and excitement at all that gorgeous, firm, brown skin cocked and ready for action. When they took off, the women's thighs pushed them forward, lifting their legs high and then coming to earth with stunning rhythm.

Tonique was wonderful to look at but not a great runner. She finished fourth in a field of eight. Not terrible, but not Olympic quality, either. She didn't seem overly disappointed and, in fact, flashed a smile at a teammate who came in second. I moved down from my seat toward the field, keeping my eye on her as she packed her gear in a small bag and headed toward the lockers. I knew I had one chance.

"Tonique?" I said. "Could I speak to you a moment?" I held out my business card. She took it from me and looked at it. The story could have ended there. She could have brushed me off or just palmed the card, granted me a fake smile, and been onto the rest of her life. Instead she said the magic words: "Do you manage the guy who sang the national anthem?"

"Yes, I do."

"Okay. If you'll wait for me to shower, we can talk."

"My pleasure."

An hour later we were sitting in a central Philly restaurant, having a vegetarian feast and talking about music. It turned out Tonique ran track but her true love was singing. "One of the reasons I came to Temple was that Philly was such a good music city," she explained, and then her full lips took in a spoonful of tofu and brown rice. "But the scene isn't what it used to be. Boyz II Men is the only game in town right now and it's been hard getting into that camp.

"So I sing around town in a socca bad, which gives me extra cash. I consider myself more Whitney Houston than Anita Baker." Tonique was pretty savvy about the business. She'd thought a lot about where she fit into the marketplace. Yet until we'd met, she hadn't met anybody credible in the music game. So I told her my background. Told her about Plush Management. Told her about the care and feeding of Brian Barnes.

I also didn't mind telling her how stunning I thought she was and how good she'd look in a video. She told me how flattered she was since I surely met many beautiful women in my travels. We were vibing each other with that strange mix of professional need and sexual subtext that marks the entertainment biz.

"I'm dying to hear your voice," I finally said.

"And I'd love to play my demos for you."

"Okay."

"But I have to make a call."

Tonique walked over to the pay phone, which was against the wall a table away from where we sat. I strained to overhear while acting like I wasn't paying attention. She told somebody (I assume it was her boyfriend) about coming in fourth. She told him she was getting something to eat. She told him she was out with friends. Told him she'd see him later. Told him she missed him. I just quietly smiled to myself and finished my tofu burger.

Her dorm room on the Temple campus was dominated by framed posters of Whitney, Aretha, and Billie Holiday. Track and field was not what Tonique dreamed about at night. She aspired to divadom. A long, narrow bed ran beneath a window that faced the Philly skyline. I sat on the edge of the bed as Tonique slipped her demo into the DAT player.

"I'm so nervous," she said.

"Don't be nervous, beautiful. Play the tape and come sit next to me."

Tonique's voice was, thankfully, quite strong in a grand diva way. I wouldn't have to lie about her singing, as she did a nice "Greatest Love of All," an okay original R&B tune, and a dance track with a Loose Ends U.K. feel that I enjoyed. I liked her voice and loved her looks. Tonique suddenly seemed like a potential client and not just an extremely hot sista.

"What do you think?" she asked, looking at me with those long eyelashes flapping like fans. I told her the truth and she leaned over and hugged me, which I hadn't expected. I let her melt into me and felt her strong arms surround my body. I could smell cocoa butter on her skin and hair. I didn't wanna be sleazy, but the longer she held me and the deeper her hug, the more things started stirring below.

"Tonique?" I whispered in her ear.

"Yes?"

"You do have a boyfriend."

"Yes, I'm seeing someone."

"I thought so."

"But they're not like you."

Now who was playing who? No question, I'd been the aggressor in reaching out to her. But now I was a ticket to fulfill a dream. I was the one who could be useful now. If this was to be an exchange, well, I was going to make sure I gave my full share.

So I pushed my head away from her shoulder. I looked into her eyes and then kissed those amazing lips. They were so big I felt like I was floating on them. My hands reached under her shirt and touched those carved muscles. I leaned my head down and found the crease of her neck, the front of her chest, and then her right and left breast.

I wanted her thighs around my head. I wanted my hands on those butt cheeks. I pulled down her sweatpants and shoved aside her panties. I felt her thighs against my ears. I put my hands around those great, powerful legs. I rested them on my shoulders. Her pussy was wet and deep; her hair down there was thick and moist. I fed in a frenzy, letting her juice spill onto my beard, letting those thighs crush my head.

Tonique looked down at me. She grabbed my head in both hands, pushing my mouth harder against her clit. Her head went back and she let loose a low note that filled her little room. Over Tonique's head I could see Whitney's poster and imagined my tongue licking her tight little pussy, too.

I stuck my hands in my pants and began jerking myself off to the taste of Tonique/Whitney. Tonique hit more notes. Tonique shook. I jerked. I licked. I struggled for breath, I nearly suffocated. I didn't care. I licked harder, deeper, faster. Pre-cum dribbled out of my dick and onto my hands. Tonique pushed my head away and leaned back into the bed. Her thighs let go of my head. I took deep, full breaths. I laid my head on one of those brown, thick, moist, lush thighs. This, I knew, was the start of a beautiful friendship.

chapter 9
North Carolina Raises Up!

Our van pulled up to the back of the club in Charlotte, sending a fat rat scurrying out into the darkness, away from two overflowing garbage cans. A tattered old poster for Waylon Jennings hung by the red backstage door. Some redneck had stuck a Confederate flag sticker next to the doorknob.

"Yo, where you got me, Dark?" Brian asked, as he reluctantly exited our vehicle.

"Believe me, black folks know where Tubby's is," I reassured him. Brian got more comfortable once we'd entered the clean, well-maintained backstage area. He was even more relaxed when he saw that the dressing room was decorated with photos of Tyrone Davis and Johnnie Taylor, as well as George Jones and Willie Nelson.

I told him, "This used to be a redneck-only spot up until the eighties when Tubby himself died and his son and daughter-in-law took over the spot and began integrating the bookings. Now this is the premier venue for black acts in the Carolinas."

Brian appreciated the history lesson, but he really perked up when a taller version of Dolly Parton walked in and said, sweet as could be, "How you boys doin'?" This unexpected visitor had a big blonde halo of holdover eighties hair, bright blue contact lens–enhanced eyes, and a small mouth hallowed in red lipstick. Blue pumps, blue jeans, and a tight, partly unbuttoned red-and-white-checkered blouse. The top three buttons were open to revealed pale mountains of flesh. Not a day under thirty-five and not ready to acknowledge it.

Her name was Lorraine Mathias, the aforementioned daughter-in-law, who was now handling day-to-day operations at Tubby's. Her husband, Tubby's son, was apparently spending most of his time running their growing real-estate business. As Lorraine related all this information, Brian and I struggled to maintain eye contact with her and not stare at her impressive breasts. But she really got our attention when she reported, "You boys should be mighty proud. The walkup sales today suggest we'll be at or near capacity."

Sony and I had spent a lot of time and money aimed

at breaking "After the Dance" in the Carolinas. The region was considered "a breakout market," where hits that would later catch the ear of programmers in bigger cities were born. To get records in the small AM stations of the South, you used friendship, gifts—financial, sexual, and pharmaceutical—and promotion (two local jocks were hosting tonight's gig and getting a cut of the door). The plan was working. The local radio was banging our record. I was really loving my new friend Lorraine.

But that feeling of fellowship was short-lived. Tubby's was a renovated field house with high ceilings and a big dance floor ringed by two long bars. That in itself wasn't the problem. But, at least to my ears, the room was a big echo chamber that could dilute the impact of bass and drums, making them seem muddy and washed out. I told Lorraine that for a club clocking major dollars off black music, the acoustics of Tubby's still seemed better suited to the less rhythmically demanding sounds of country and western.

During the soundcheck we both stood behind the sound board checking the levels and arguing. Tonight was likely the first time Brian would be playing before a crowd coming expressly to see him. They may have come because of a hot record, but I wanted them to leave as fans of the man, not bitching he sounded better on the record.

As Brian came off stage I spotted a tall, brown beauty, a handsome high-yellow brother, a photographer,

DARK

96

and a middle-age black bureaucrat carrying a sign, all standing in the wings aiming anxious eyes at me. The beauty, wisely, spoke first.

"Mr. Dark, my name is Desiree Washington. I am the reigning Miss North Carolina and I came today to ask you and your client a favor." She was five foot nine in high heels, tapered black slacks, and a red blouse generously opened at the top. A gold necklace decorated her supple-looking neck. Her hair was thick and jet black. Her haunting brown eyes were a shade or two lighter than her flawless mocha skin. Her smile was so bright I started to reach for my sunglasses. If the favor was wanting my first-born child, consider that a deal.

She continued with her rap: "I am the spokesperson for the state's sickle cell anemia foundation and I wondered if Brian Barnes could take a picture with me and our sign?"

My answer would normally be no. I don't just let my clients get associated with a charitable organization I know nothing about. But for this fine-ass woman, of course. Which, of course, was Desiree's plan all along.

Desiree introduced me to her posse, the most significant member being Dwight Murdock, a square-jawed, square-headed, light-skinned brother who served as her manager and her boyfriend. Dwight had the firm handshake and cocky bearing of the former high school football star he once was. Now he was in law school and about to take the bar.

All of which made Brian hate him. Like natural ene-mies, the R&B star and the handsome ex-jock eyed each other across the dressing room, which was clearly not big enough for both of them and Desiree. She felt the tension immediately and deflected it with a smile and praise for Brian's "wonderful record" and "sweet voice." As they stood looking pretty for the cameraman, I saw Brian's hand slide down her waist and cup one of her lovely ass cheeks. Desiree didn't give it away. Her smile didn't change. I glanced over to Dwight to see if he'd noticed, but he hadn't. So I didn't have to referee.

After Desiree and company left (with free tickets in their pockets), all Brian could talk about was Desiree—her eyes, her lips, the way her ass felt in his hand. "I'm gonna get that girl, Dark. After my show tonight it's on. That square-head country boy can't hang with me. He just better be ready to get his feelings hurt."

"Cool," I said, "Channel all that energy into your per-formance tonight and Dwight won't be a problem." I ac-tually didn't think Desiree would dump a handsome lawyer for a traveling musician (even for one night). She knew her value too well to do that, and especially after he'd treated her like a groupie by grabbing her ass. But I didn't say that to Brian. I liked him feeling like the cock of the walk. Let him bring that to the stage tonight.

I guided him to the tour bus and sent him and the band off to the hotel for a nap and a shower. I decided to chill in the dressing room, using my cell and the club's phone to make multiple calls. I talked to Sony. To a possi-ble road manager named Bobby Duck. To Chi Chi about doing choreography for Brian "at a discount," since she already had a piece of the deal. I spoke to Tonique, who was at a track meet in Delaware. After all those calls, and a few others, I rested my head on the dressing-room table and fell into a dream.

I was a cloud, a huge, thick, black cloud heavy with moisture. I floated over a lush, green field filled with lovely, luscious naked women. They laid on the grass looking up at me, their breasts quivering, their gaze ador-ing, their legs crossed and then wide, wide open. I floated down and covered the green field in a fine mist. My moisture wet their arms, legs, and their lips. First they were all lightly sprinkled with my essence and then I en-veloped them in my darkness.

"Dark!"

A voice awakened me. Lorraine looked down at me from a great height, it seemed.

"Sorry to disturb you, darlin', but there's something' you need to see."

It was like a vision from the dream, except everyone had their clothes on. A long line of people, mostly women, mostly black, stood on line to enter Tubby's. Short, tall, Lean Cuisine, and supersize, all these women had their purses open and their eyes twinkling. All were in line to see Brian Barnes. A few even clutched copies of the poster and album. There had been reports from Sony's merchandisers that Brian's pretty young face was being stolen out of retailers across the country. But this line was the first truly tangible confirmation that real people, not just DJs on payola, were excited.

"Thanks for waking me," I said to Lorraine. "This is even better than my dream."

"Well, that's somethin', considerin' . . ."

"Considering what?"

"That your dream sounded wonderful. Somethin' about moist skin."

I hadn't been embarrassed in quite some time, but I felt the blood rushing to my face right then.

"Don't you worry," she said with an amused smile. "I won't tell a soul. But you do have to share with me later."

"Okay," I said, hoping to put the topic behind me. I wasn't sure if this was real flirting or just some polite ass kissing because of the all the money my client was making for Lorraine.

But ninety minutes later I wasn't worried about Lorraine or my dreams or sleep, 'cause I was knee deep in the present and very confident about the future. Brian Barnes was onstage and the crowd was in rapture.

"We love you!" a chubby sista screamed.

"Give it to me!" a thin lady in braids wailed.

"I'm having your baby!" a light-skinned woman sporting one of America's last heads of Jheri Curls shouted.

This wasn't the night that Brian Barnes sang his best

or danced his best or even seemed most confident (I could tell the crowd's intensity scared him a bit). This was the first night the crowd was ready for him. They'd heard him on the radio, seen his picture in *Right On!* and *Jet.* They peeped his interview on BET. They were smitten. They came to see if she would receive their love and how he gave his. Was he warm or aloof? A romantic Romeo or a cold-hearted playa? A little boy or a mack? And, like any true love man, Brian was all these things—sometimes all at the same time. They'd hoped he'd deliver a benediction; he just wanted their blessing.

At the side of the stage, in a little VIP area, alongside the wife and daughter of the local black congressman, the owner of the local Lincoln Mercury dealership, and a slew of radio station personnel was Desiree and Dwight. She was swaying to the music. Her boyfriend stood with one foot tapping, clearly liking the music but in no mood to give real love. I wondered if she'd come backstage with Dwight later or would she, somehow, come back by herself, having dumped her man to touch the hem of Brian's garment.

I was basking in Brian's glow when I felt someone come close to me at the soundboard.

"I didn't know he'd be this good."

"So Lorraine, you wanna add a second show?"

"Oh, so you're a mind reader, too?"

"It only makes sense, but I'll only agree to it if we get a bump on our guarantee. Tomorrow's crowd won't be as big, but then that's not my problem if you want him again."

"Slow down, cowboy," Lorraine said into my ear, leaning in a lot closer than necessary. "You got the goods. No need for hard ball. When you come to pick up your money tonight, we'll make arrangements." As she was leaving, I felt a small hand squeeze my butt. Lorraine just kept walking like nothing had happened. I looked to see if any of the Tubby's staff had seen her move. Fucking a married Southern white woman in her place of business didn't seem like a good idea.

Once the show was over I collected Brian from the stage and hustled him back to the dressing room. There I assigned Sony's local promotional rep the job of door management. Until I came back from Lorraine's office he was in charge of deciding who would and would not gain access to Brian. And I told him—not only pretty girls. Let the girls who don't usually get to kiss the prince come in to see him, too. Once smitten, they make the truest fans.

Lorraine was sitting behind her desk. In front of her was a brown paper bag containing our share of the gate. Standing next to the desk was a burly, big-headed guy with a mullet and a gut. He wore a stretched-out Tubby's T-shirt and jeans that had seen better days.

"So," I said, "you wanna negotiate terms for the extra show."

"I already spoke to your bookin' agent in New York."

"Really?"

"You're not the only person who knows how to take care of business."

"Okay. I hear that." I reached under my shirt and pulled out my money belt, which I'd had wrapped around my waist.

"Larry? Could you excuse us a minute," she said to her employee. "I need to discuss a few things with Mr. Dark. Why don't you go keep Brian Barnes's door secure."

"You sure, Lorraine?" he said skeptically. "You know, Matty—"

"Matty isn't your boss. I am."

After Lorraine gave the verbal smackdown, Larry shuffled out, cutting me a hard "don't gloat at me, nigger" look. As I reached for the bag, Lorraine snatched it from me. A big, nasty grin took control of her ruby red lips.

"You are a control freak, aren't ya, darlin'?"

I reached for the bag and she pulled it away again.

"Yo, anybody tell you not to mess with a man's money?"

"No. But I've heard never mess with a nigger's money."

At that I stood up, came around the desk, and jerked her to her feet.

"Don't play with me, woman. I don't care who you are or where we're at. I'll slap that silly look right off your pale, white, over-madeup face."

She looked at me a little scared, a little excited. She

leaned in and I felt those huge breasts up against my chest.

"I'm sorry, Dark. I shouldn't have said that."

"Damn right."

I let her go. She held up the bag of money and then poured the bills out onto the floor.

"What now, bitch!?"

She answered by dropping to her knees, using the spilled money as a cushion.

"What are you doing?" I said, though it was pretty clear what she wanted to do.

"I love," she said as she placed her red-nailed hands on my hips, "a cocky man. Especially one who'll be out of town in two days."

"You trying to get me lynched?"

"This is the new South, Dark."

Lorraine placed her face next to my crotch and then used her teeth to slowly pull down my zipper. Clearly this lady was in the midst of a serious midlife crisis. I thought of the mean look on Larry's face. I thought of my artist waiting on me in his crowded dressing room. I thought of the money under her feet that I needed to deposit in the hotel's safe.

But you know what? Unexpected blow jobs don't come around every day. Common sense and sex are two warring aesthetics. Common sense keeps you safe from harm. It is a calm, realistic ability that allows you to see trouble, measure the cost, and avoid it. Sex doesn't have a brain—just a head. Sex is not about thought—it's all action. Sex is happy in its ignorance. It exists purely to create immediate gratification and future memories. So when Lorraine pulled at my now swollen dick and grabbed it with both hands, common sense left the room.

I looked down at my brown skin being held firmly as it slid in and out of her thin red lips. I particularly enjoyed the sight of her wedding ring moving back and forth over my dick. The idea of her violating her marital vows for a taste of me fed my ego royally. Normally it takes a while for me to come, but this Southern belle's hunger for me was so intoxicating I surprised myself by coming quickly with a loud groan. Lorraine opened her mouth and stuck out her tongue proudly, like she was displaying a hard-won trophy. Then she pulled her tongue back inside and swallowed.

"You eat a balanced diet," she observed.

"You can tell that?"

"Oh, yeah, darlin'. You are what you eat."

She scooped up the money on the floor. I pulled a money belt from around my waist, took the bills from her, and then put the belt back on.

"You've got a couple of more days in Charlotte," she said, now standing at her full height and looking me in the eye.

"That's right."

"So now you owe me a bonus."

Larry eyed us suspiciously as we exited. That look

worried me. She was the late owner's daughter-in-law and, despite this being 1990, this was still North Carolina. I glanced at Lorraine to see if this registered with her and noticed a small, shiny bit of sperm on her chin. My eyes must have revealed my concern because she wiped her face quickly.

Feeling satisfied and guilty, I moved through the crowd outside Brian's door. Inside the room a comely coed named Latia sat in Brian's lap, while her big-hipped friend Tanisha sat on a sofa sipping a Heineken, the green bottle looking lovely between her fat, brown lips. There were other folks in the room, but Brian was giving these two the most energy. Sadly there was no sign of Desiree Washington, but Brian seemed content, so I didn't bring it up.

Back at the hotel, Brian snuggled on the sofa with Latia, while Tanisha rolled a fat joint next to her. I chatted with a local label rep named Dave about the record's success in North Carolina. A couple of crew people sipped brews and chatted up some local girls. I made a hitching-a-ride motion with my thumb in Brian's direction and he nodded.

"Okay, everybody," I announced, "the party is over. Brian has to rest." I herded everyone out except, of course, Latia and Tanisha. I was about to ask Brian if he needed anything else when he stood up and began singing Marvin Gaye's "Let's Get It On."

Now this was a really corny, obvious thing to do. But

then, if I sang as well as Brian, I could get away with being that corny and obvious. In that living room Brian gave an impromptu performance that had both girls mesmerized. "You know what I'm talkin' 'bout," he sang, "c'mon, baby." The sound of a true singer's voice, unamplified, strong, and committed, can send a vibration into the air that can make your chair shake, your neck tingle, and the bones in your chest rattle and hum.

It can be a dazzling, moving, arousing experience. It led Latia to giggle, as if that girlish sound was the only way she could communicate her excitement. Tanisha was equally moved but in a totally different way, She pulled hard on her joint. Then big, huge swells of water collected in her eyes and then dropped, heavy and rich as summer fruit, onto her cheeks. A hand rose quickly to wipe them away.

By the time Brian was improvising on the tag, Latia had risen from her seat to hug the singer. As he crooned into her ear Latia began grinding up against him, like they were at a house party. Her hands found his ass and then, as if they'd flowed through the fabric, into his jeans, where one hand cupped his ass and the other grabbed his dick. With a dexterity born of desire, Latia fondled Brian's body and continued to grind against it, too.

Latia then separated from Brian, one hand still holding his body, the other unbuttoning her blouse. Brian was both active and passive, singing "Let's get it on . . . we gotta get it on . . ." with a churchy inflection, while Latia moved around him like she was collecting pieces of a particularly rewarding puzzle.

Tanisha, her eyes red and face flushed, stood behind her friend and began sliding off Latia's top. That accomplished, she undid the clasp on Latia's bra and slid it off. "Get it on . . . we gotta get it on . . ." Brian continued singing, now so softly, it was melodic whispering. Latia's round, brown breasts and large areolas swung slowly in unison with her hips.

Though unplanned and improvised, the two girls began undressing Brian in tandem, slipping off his shirt, pulling down his trousers, ripping off boxers until all he had on were his boots and a couple of gold chains around his neck. And still he sang.

By now Brian was back to the verse, whispering. Both girls, half-clothed and dreamy eyed, embraced him, rubbing Brian's skin with all four hands, kissing his limbs with both their mouths. I looked down and found my hand inside my pants. Not an hour after my negotiation with Lorraine I had a big-ass boner again. But this wasn't my party. Without a word I moved away. As Latia and Tanisha were devouring Brian, I closed the door.

Back in my room there were faxes under the door and messages on the hotel phone. I settled in to do some work when Desiree Washington's voice came through on the voicemail. "Hello, Mr. Dark, this is Desiree Washington. We met tonight at Brian Barnes's show. I hope you re-

member me." Ah, come on. Like I could forget Miss North
Carolina. "I was wondering if you were free for lunch tomorrow. My treat. I'd like to discuss my career with you.
That is, if you're interested." I hadn't encountered a
woman who played coy in quite a while. Must be that
beauty pageant training. Looked like this girl had a
dream.

The next morning I entered Brian's room with a cup
of coffee in my hand around 6:00 A.M. The living room
was a mess of half-empty beer bottles, rolling paper, and
scattered sofa cushions. Air-conditioning circulated the
scent of stale sex. Brian laid across his bed, facedown, a
pillow next to his face. The girls were nowhere in sight,
though I saw a pair of black panties dangling off the foot
of the bed. I opened the blinds and then put the coffee on
the floor near Brian's head. I shook him softly.

His eyes opened slowly and then his right hand ab-
sently massaged his balls.

"Have a good night?"

"Oh, man," he mumbled. "These country gals are
wild. But I handled by business, partner."

"Good to know," I said. "They coming back for
tonight's show?"

"I don't know, but they sure are welcome here."

Brian had thrown a towel across his waist and was
heading to the bathroom when I told him Desiree had
called me. That stopped him.

"Word up? You a mack like that?"

"No," I said, "but she might be. I'm sure I look like a ticket out of North Carolina."

"Depends on what she has to offer, right?"

"That's right," I said. "That's what it's always about. Anyway, how you feeling this morning?"

"Like shit."

"Well, take your shower quick. We have some radio interviews set up."

We sat in the hallway of Charlotte's top R&B station, waiting to go on the morning show. This was an R&B ritual. A full-on performance, a late night of women and wine, and then an morning radio interview—that's how the R&B biz worked. Many artists never went to sleep after a show. They became totally nocturnal creatures, vampires really, who slept all day, waiting to emerge from their coffins at dusk.

Brian was acclimating himself to this new lifestyle. His body was transforming—just like in that Japanese cartoon show that was so popular. My job was to smooth that transition. If by night I was sometimes Brian's pimp, by day I was his coach. The morning show team, a jolly brother and a chunky sista, were full of energy and compliments, snapping Brian awake with their good humor and banter.

Back at the hotel I tucked him in and put a DO NOT DISTURB sign on his door and a block on Brian's phone. I laid down for a couple of hours and then got up and on the phone. At 12:30 P.M. I went down to the hotel restau-

rant and inside, looking as prim and proper as the debu-
tante she was, sat Desiree Washington. She kissed my
cheek and hugged me warmly. After I sat down Desiree
handed me a manila envelope that contained her head
shot.

"I'm an actress," she said. Her credits were mostly
collegiate and some local summer stock theater. She had
performed a one-woman show at the black theater festival in Winston-Salem playing Harriet Tubman. "I want
you to manage me."

"I'm not really prepared to do that," I told her. "I've
always thought I'd like to do TV and film eventually, but
I'm not at that point right now."

"But you will be one day. Brian is gonna be a star, I
could see that from the reaction of the crowd. That's
going to open the door to a lot of opportunities for you
as his manager."

"You thought about this last night?"

"It hit me during the show."

"So you liked him?"

"He sings and moves well onstage but, honestly, I'm
not turned on by a man who pinches the ass of a woman
he's just met."

"I saw that."

"I know you did. I'm sure some of these groupies he
meets on the road feel flattered by that kind of attention.
I am not one of those girls."

"That's very clear."

"Anyway, what about managing me? I know I have the skills and I think I'm attractive enough for film or TV."

"Think you're attractive enough? Come on, Miss North Carolina."

She handed me a VHS tape of her one-woman show and said, "I know you'll be impressed." We talked more about her love of acting and her plans to move to Los Angeles in a few months. That's how it works. The most beautiful girl in her hometown or even her whole state gets restless and decides, or rather her ego decides, it's time to conquer the world. Most of them end up back home married to the biggest local car dealer or banker. Some end up marrying a Hollywood type—a personal trainer to the stars, a dentist to the studio heads, etc. A lucky few end up on a soap opera or even network TV. The unfortunate few end up stripping or making pornos out in the Valley. One in a million becomes Halle Berry. Whichever fate awaited Desiree Washington, I suspected she saw me as a possible way out of state.

"Let me look at the tape," I said. "We'll talk after I see it." Before she left Desiree, kissed my cheek again and hugged me warmly one more time. I watched her fine self walk out of the hotel and wondered if she'd play a bigger role in my life.

She didn't come to the next show at Tubby's—she had to visit a hospital for a sickle cell fund-raiser. The girl had good values, no doubt. The crowd was much smaller than the previous night, but about a third had come back from the night before—real Brian Barnes fans. I got as many addresses as I could, knowing folks like these could be the backbone of the fan club I wanted to start.

After that night's show I received a deep soul kiss from Lorraine just before she tried to cut into my share of the gate, claiming the crowd was disappointing. To spare a lot of time negotiating, I finger fucked her in her office and (again, at her request) licked that finger slowly in front of her. Larry looked at me real hard again when I walked out and I knew it was time to leave Charlotte. Brian's two college conquests from the night before tried to slip into the tour bus and ride down to Atlanta with us to Freaknik, but I vetoed that plan.

As the bus cut across the state line into South Carolina on the way to Atlanta, I nervously slipped Desiree's tape into the VCR. "You gonna watch it with me?" I asked Brian, who was leafing through *Billboard*.

"She didn't wanna get with me, so why should I care if she can act?"

"You're not curious at all?"

"I got no time for games, Dark. I see how this star shit goes down. I really don't have to chase anymore, so why should I?"

"It keeps you humble."

"But you don't want me to be humble, do you?"

"Good point," I admitted.

"I can't wait to go down to Freaknik. I'm going to

sleep now and get my rest." With that my suddenly diligent student disappeared into the back bedroom. So I watched Desiree Washington as she tried to look like a crusty old ex-slave rebel. She didn't look the part but was damn moving in the role anyway. She was beautiful and she could act. But in L.A. those qualities were a dime a dozen. I fell asleep with her tape playing.

chapter 10
Peachtree Peaches

This is a fucking dope idea," Brian said, and punched me in the arm.

"Ouch," I replied as the Brian Barnes tour bus turned into the campus of Atlanta's Spelman College, the nation's premier all-black women's college known for quality academics and some of the finest light, bright coeds in the country. The good idea wasn't simply to drive across Spelman's campus, which blooded touring musicians had done for years, but to have an arranged record signing at the Spelman bookstore. Not only would we attract Spelman young ladies from their dorms, but since the school was located in Atlanta University Center, aka the AU Center, along with the colleges of Morris

Brown, Clark, and Morehouse, we'd pull kids from all four schools.

Besides, making an appearance at Spelman would separate us from Freaknik, the spring break bacchanal that went on every year in the ATL. It had started as an annual gathering of fraternities and sororities in the Peachtree City, but had evolved in the eighties into a black collegiate freakathon with all the debauchery and drug use that suggests. By the end of the nineties the city fathers (and mothers) had had enough of the street craziness and basically shut Freaknik down.

But in that year Freaknik was still in full effect and we were in town anxious to bite a Georgia peach or two. As we came across the Spelman campus, we'd seen groups of teenagers, mostly girls, carrying copies of Brian's CD, his cassette, posters, or copies of *Black Beat* with Brian's picture on the cover. They'd see the bus or wave or run or just scream. The most enthused started to chase us, jogging behind the bus and yelling my client's name.

Not yet jaded by the attention, Brian went to the window and waved at his fans, looking as excitedly juvenile as they did. Showbiz makes teenagers of people in the game, 'cause on some level your business is play—parties, concerts, all-nighters, travel. For nine-to-five folks this stuff is the ice cream and cake of life, for show folk it's the staple of our existence. Plus the sex. Show-biz grants everyone involved license to be free, to experiment, to bask in dirty impulses and naughty deeds. And, of course, that's especially true if you live at the center of the storm. Brian was evolving into a living, breathing embodiment of its eye, its calm sexy center around which all the tempest swirls.

My mentoree was living in this moment with a big smile and a young, hard dick. Few men get to be so desired. Few black men are ever this treasured. Some of the girls screamed, "I love you, Brian Barnes!" at him, but those were just words. "Love" maybe. "Lust" definitely.

At the small scholarly Spelman bookstore, where photos of Alice Walker, Toni Morrison, and Fannie Lou Hamer adorned the walls, young women lined up to kiss Brian, slip him their dorm room number, and take pictures of him as if he were Michael Jackson circa 1979. His record was being blasted all over Atlanta radio and was starting to move out of record bins.

While most of the coeds rolled in and out, individual girls and a couple of groups lingered, not moving on as the security guards suggested, but instead staying close to the signing area. There was one particularly striking trio of Alpha Kappa Alpha girls, dressed in the color of their sorority and in three short skirts, standing stage left, looking very poised and quite delicious. I gave Brian a nod, and he shook his head yes, so I walked over to introduce myself. Condi, Anna, and Pamela were juniors who had pledged together. Condi and Anna had been in the same Jack & Jill chapter back in Chicago.

Condi and Anna had pretty orange-toned complexions and brunette hair, while Pamela was light brown with a round face and full lips. Condi had a haughty poise, while Anna and Pamela looked more relaxed. Anna and Condi looked a touch interchangeable—same height, same look—though Condi's lashes were longer and she had more freckles around her nose.

I invited them to accompany us to the hotel to get to know Brian. Pamela was with it immediately, while her sorority pals asked if Brian had a girlfriend (as if an affirmative answer was gonna stop them from getting on the damn bus). I could see that Condi and Anna wanted to be wined and dined, while Pamela, who seemed to be a bit of a third wheel, wasn't gonna be held back by peer pressure. She was the darkest of the three, so perhaps she felt some pressure to compete with her friends for men. As any experienced man can tell you, this kind of competitive tension between girlfriends is very exploitable.

"Ladies, if you're coming with us, I suggest you make up your minds, 'cause as soon as this signing is over we're jetting out of here to a radio interview on V-One-oh-three."

"Well," Pamela announced, "I'm going," which put pressure on her peers. Condi and Anna caved. Like they were gonna let Pamela have all the fun.

Getting Brian out of the bookstore had a couple of hairy moments—one little girl grabbed Brian around the neck, trying to kiss him and almost threw out his back.

Thankfully a security guard scooped her up before my man got a hernia.

On the bus Brian sat across from Condi, Anna, and Pamela with his body slumped on the sofa and his legs wide open. His eyes surveyed the three young ladies slowly and lustfully. Condi and Anna sat perfectly poised, like little girls playing at the gestures of womanhood. Pamela was cooler. She sat slightly away from them and leafed through a copy of *Jet* magazine that featured Brian in the Week's Best Photos section. But when she did look at Brian it was with a very adult intensity. The other two seemed outwardly more sophisticated but there was a mature carnality to Pamela that Brian didn't miss.

"What you thinking about, Pamela?" he asked.

She replied, "About how you're gonna dedicate a song to me tomorrow night," which made him and me both laugh.

"Is that what I'm gonna do?" Brian said. "You sound real cocky right now, you know?"

"I am," she shot back.

"Why am I gonna dedicate a song to you and not Condi or Anna?"

"No disrespect," she replied, "but they don't have it going on quite like I do."

Her two sorority sisters were both pissed off by Pamela's reply, but I could see this young lady was in it to win it.

"Baby, you raw," Brian said approvingly.

"Takes someone raw to see someone raw," she said back. Brian was cracking up now. Pamela was bold and wasn't afraid to show it.

At V-103, Atlanta's biggest urban station, Brian let Pamela sit in the studio with him as he did an on-air interview. Condi and Anna cooled their heels in an outer studio with me. As the interview unfolded I made calls and watched the two snooty college girls quietly fume. I walked over to them and asked, "Did Brian offer you tickets to tomorrow's show?"

"No," Condi said haughtily, "he did not."

"Well, I'm not sure I even wanna go," Anna replied. "His taste in women is questionable."

"Let me give you girls a bit of advice. If you wanna get with a star like Brian, you can't be shy about letting him know."

"We are not stunts, Mr. Dark." Condi had some steel in her.

Anna was softer, saying, "I don't think you were saying we had to be as aggressive as Pamela, were you?"

Anna stared at me with her hazel eyes. She was locked into me. She was separating herself from Condi, letting me know she was making herself available.

I replied, "No. Not necessarily. Your friend was just more assertive, that's all. I mean, you girls knew enough to get on the bus with us. You wanted access to this world. Well, you got it. I'll make sure you both have tickets for tomorrow night."

"What," Anna said as she touched my hand, "about backstage passes?"

"Well," I said smoothly, "I'll have to see."

"Aren't you the manager?"

"Yes, I am."

Condi, feeling left out, cut in with, "Can't you see he's playing you?"

"It's all play," I said to both of them. "This isn't real life. It's the circus. We just rolled into town to put up the big top. If you wanna enjoy the show, you can. But don't make it what it's not. I'm the ring master. You wanna put your head in the lion's mouth or do you wanna just sit in the stands?"

Anna squeezed my hand tight. "You sure talk a lot of shit, don't you, Dark?"

"This is what I do. Day and night."

After the interview Anna peeled off from Condi and took my arm as we walked back to the bus. Up close she smelled a little floral, like a garden of flowers, and her voice was young and soft as she whispered that she thought I was sexy.

Back on the bus Brian, Condi, and Pamela stared as Anna slowly tongue kissed me on the sofa. Pamela held Brian's hand and smiled as I toured the soft contours of Anna's young mouth. Like a lot of young women, she sometimes moved too quickly. I took her face in my hands and slowed her down. Then I pressed the tip of my tongue against the top of hers and then onto the plump inside of her lips. I kissed her slightly open mouth and felt her heart pumping faster through her blouse. When I came up for air I could see Brian and Pamela were petting heavily across from us with Pamela's hands all down his pants.

Condi? She sat far away from us with her arms folded across her chest, looking disgusted at the whole scene.

Once we reached the Omni I had to switch back to manager mode, overseeing our check-in, making sure that our crew members were taken care of, and grabbing a handul of faxes from Sony. Since I had work to do I suggested the girls roll up to Brian's room. Of course Condi was ready to go back to campus, but her two friends were going nowhere. I left them to negotiate amongst themselves. I'd already had a little fun and now felt I should actually be earning my money.

Once I checked us into our rooms I switched on the local news radio station, which was filled with reports about the influx of young people into the city. Parties were scheduled everywhere. Traffic was expected to slow to a crawl outside the AU Center, in Buckhead, by the Lenox Mall, and especially at the park, which was the epicenter of Freaknik. I was on the phone with the promoter of the Omni concert when there was a knock on my door. Condi stood there, looking despondent.

"What's wrong?"

"They're in with Brian," she said sadly.

"In with Brian, huh?"

Guess Anna didn't wanna wait on me. Well, I was trying to make the man a sex symbol. Anna moving on to Brian was a sign it was working. And she was real young. Now I had Condi standing in front of me looking disappointed (either in her friends or herself or both). I thought it was odd that Condi hadn't just taken a cab back to campus, but I let her in anyway and pointed to the sofa.

I got back on the phone as Condi sat on the sofa looking forlorn and, I must say, quite succulent, with her lips stuck out and her hazel eyes cloudy. I motioned to the minibar and suggested she help herself. I moved my calls into the bedroom, where I haggled with various people for about twenty minutes or so. When I finally hung up I saw Condi standing by the door with a drink in her hand—smelled like Jack Daniel's cut with water—and no shoes on her slim, beautifully pedicured, perfectly shaped feet.

"Would you like something to drink?"

"Yeah, sure," I said, pleasantly surprised. "A beer would be nice, but not an American brand."

From where I sat I could see Condi walk over and then bend down to open the minibar. That short skirt she had on clinched up and around her hips in the most pleasing way, and the curve of her butt was outlined by brilliantly white panties. Condi had a small waist that swept out to lovely hips and wonderful thighs. Her legs were a little thick, but that was fine since they looked like they might soon be balancing on my shoulders. Condi walked back toward me with languid looseness and handed me a beer bottle.

"They only have Miller," she said, handing me the bottle and staring at me with slightly inebriated intensity. "But you should be having a real drink anyway."

"Little girl, that smells like Jack Daniel's. It's not even five o'clock. You sure you know what you're doing?"

"My daddy taught me how to drink. He said, 'If you can hold your liquor no man can take advantage of you.' If you can hold it together drinking JD, you can hold it down drinking anything."

"Your daddy was a wise man," I said as I sucked down some beer and then placed the bottle on the floor.

I ran my eyes up and down her young body. I reached up with both my hands and pulled her freckled face close to mine.

"So," I asked, "are you drunk or just relaxed?"

Condi kinda laughed, kinda smirked at my comment. She pulled her face out of my hands and then sat on the edge of the desk. "I just met you not three hours ago. Why should I sleep with you?" She was challenging me and not being shy about it. I stood up so that I looked down at her, my eyes on hers. My hands reached down to clasp her slim fingers in mine.

"There is no reason in the world, Condi. Other than it would be damn good. That's the only reason to do anything."

I leaned my face down to hers and pressed my lips against hers. Then I pushed my tongue through her reluctant lips and into her mouth until she yielded to me, sucking me in deep and warm. Using my hands I raised her chin up and savored the blend of strawberry-flavored lipstick and the tart kick of Jack Daniel's.

Young girls sometimes don't know their own minds. They teeter between the morality of the "right and wrong" they were taught and the adult passion they desire. I wasn't sure how far Condi would go but I was prepared to back off when she found her limit. My senses were looking for any sign of resistance as I took her into my arms, feeling her lean, supple body against mine and engulfing her.

The JD had loosened Condi up and the idea that her friends were likely getting busy obviously had some effect on her. All she might have wanted now was the validation of her sex appeal and not actually sex. I was very aware young girls could be real skittish. I was about fifteen years her elder, so I had to tread carefully. My tongue stung from the taste of a fruity perfume on her thin neck. She moaned softly and cradled my head with her hands. I reached down and cupped one of her round ass cheeks in one hand and then, through her dress, pushed two fingers between her legs. Through those white lace panties I could feel a welcome moistness.

Using the index finger and thumb of my left hand, I

popped her bra open, then I pushed it down and placed my mouth on one of her breasts. Her nipples were surrounded by a wide areola, which I nibbled softly with my teeth. She squeezed my head in her hands. Her strong breath pulsed through her body. I shoved faxes and papers off the desk and onto the floor, lifting Condi onto the table. I pushed her dress up above her hips and brought my head down between her legs. Not even bothering to take her panties off, I just slid them to the side and brought my lips to hers.

Condi clutched my head like a life raft. I dived in for dear life. I don't know when young Condi had last had her pussy eaten, but I'm sure it wasn't done before by anyone who knew what they were doing. Hairy and tender and needy, Condi's pussy opened itself up to me. Her clit danced for me, moving in quick, dizzying circles. The phone rang. I threw it to the floor. Condi's head banged against the wall behind the desk. She didn't seem to care. Her nails squeezed my head. One leg pressed hard against my shoulder and back. Long, wicked moans filled the room. She was almost there.

And then I walked away, stopped, and stood erect. I didn't touch Condi or even speak to her. I just walked over to the bed, undressed slowly, and then sat on the edge of it with my dick in my right hand. With young women you gotta make things clear. It was gonna be her decision to take it to the next level. I just looked at her.

She walked over to me. She dropped her dress and panties to the floor. Her brown hair was matted to her forehead with sweat.

And then she kneeled before me and took me in both hands and into her lovely, young mouth. She wasn't that experienced in oral sex but her enthusiasm was enough to make my dick enlarge to full length and heft. I watched myself move in and out of Condi's mouth before I finally had to stop before I exploded. She sat on the bed next to me and we kissed, me tasting my dick and she tasting her pussy.

"I'm on the pill," she whispered. Those magic words have caused more heartache than any in the English language save for "I love you."

"That's good," I said. Still, I bent down to dig a condom out of my wallet. Only then, after I'd wrapped myself up, did I enter young Condi. I'd like to brag that I turned homegirl out, but this wasn't the best fucking of my life. I think Condi was, on some level, still very uncomfortable, thinking more about what she was doing than actually doing it. After about twenty minutes I stopped and just held her in my arms.

We were silent a while and then I wondered aloud if she wanted to shower with me.

"Yeah," she said, "I'd like that."

So I picked her up in my arms and carried her into the bathroom. Like an old married couple we washed each other's bodies, carefully cleaning the spots we'd made dirty and feeling the places we'd just nibbled on each other.

"I've never done that before," she said as we toweled off.

"Which part?"

"None of it," she said. Her eyes looked a little teary. "I mean, not with a man I just met a few hours before. I mean, I'm not sure I even like you."

I stopped drying her off and looked her in the eye. "So, how do you feel right now, Condi? Tell me the truth." I was worried that we were adding up to a nasty equation. Young girl + older man + hotel room + alcohol = BIG TROUBLE.

She smiled weakly. "I actually feel really nice." She hugged me, placing her head against my chest. I sighed with relief. Then, with her head still pressed against me, she asked, "But what will I tell Pamela and Anna?"

I whispered to her, "You'll tell them we had lunch and at first I was surprisingly sweet. And that I plied you with hard liquor and tried to seduce you and you told me to kiss your sweet young ass. That's all they need to know."

"Our secret, right?"

"Just me, you, and that desk ever have to know."

Reassured, Condi dressed quickly, heading back to campus with plenty of cab fare in her pocket and two tickets for the show in her lovely hands. My encounter with Condi had really been unexpected and, though not really great sex, there was something sweet about how it went down (at least for me). Figuring Brian and his two newest friends had had a more energetic time I went down to his room and let myself in. Sitting in the living room were Anna and Pamela, both fully clothed and bored, watching MTV.

"Where's Brian?"

"We don't know," Pamela said with a pout.

"He went out to get ice," Anna explained, "but he never came back." The college girls told me he'd been gone about an hour. Sensing a problem I told the girls they had to leave, promised them tickets to the show (but no taxi fare), and then called hotel security. Where the hell was my star?

chapter 11
Visual Peaches

I walked up and down the hallway—no sign of Brian Barnes. I looked down over the hotel's inner balcony into the lobby—no sign of Brian Barnes. I was tired from my unexpected episode with Condi, but Brian's absence was filling me with anxious anxiety. What makes a would-be pop star leave two coeds alone in his hotel room? My years on the road gave me one answer: a sexier offer.

I went down to the front desk and asked to speak to the hotel's head of security. He was a big, brown waterlemon-head brother named Ned Goines. He had eyes that said he'd seen a lot of strange things and liked most of it. I ran down my concerns. He listened, nodded, and then went and made a couple of phone calls.

"I found him," Ned said with a hint of a smile on his round lips. "Go to suite eleven nineteen. You'll find who you're looking for and then some."

"What does that mean?"

"It's all under control, Mr. Dark," he replied. "We're both men of the world."

I took the elevator up to the eleventh floor with all kinds of scenarios running through my head. If it had been a serious security issue Goines would have come up with me. If it was just some girl Brian had met randomly, how would Goines have known whom to call? I got off the elevator and walked slowly toward a room at the far end of the hallway. When I got close to the door I heard loud fucking sounds (bed squeaking, people moaning, bodies smacking with sweat). I put my ear to it and heard a familiar voice saying breathlessly, "Do that shit, baby. Yeah, do it."

I knocked on the door hard and firm, like a hotel detective. Voices on the other side of the door either went silent or went "Shhhhhh!" or said, "Be quiet! Be quiet!"

"I'm looking for Brian Barnes!" I shouted. "This is his manager."

Hushed hectic conversation and the fast movement of feet could be heard. Someone came to the door and cracked it open slightly. I saw an eyeball. The door opened more. A sweaty brown face looked at me. My star.

"Yo, Dark, we got something going on here!" he said in a whisper.

"And that is?"

Brian looked over his shoulder and shrugged.

"You better let me come in," I said.

Brian was shirtless with his pants unbuckled and his underwear showing (this was years before it became official urban style). He led me past a bathroom with a wet floor and a funky smell, down a short hallway into a room cluttered with lights, discarded clothes, a half-eaten bucket of KFC, and a twenty-something brother with a camcorder. On a queen-size bed were three naked people—two big-butt college-age girls and a dude with the longest damn dick I'd ever seen, which both girls were happily feeding from.

In about a year Clarence Thomas's porn collection would make Long Dong Silver a household name. Well, in that hotel room I was witnessing a black man living up to every stereotype of the race and then add three inches! Now, I'm as heterosexual as the next brother, but damn, I had to watch this man in awe for a few moments. One girl had the tip in her mouth; the other was licking back and forth along the shaft like it was a thick, brown icicle. The brother, whose name I later learned was Lexington Steele, stood with his hands on his hips, occasionally smiling at the camera and often bending his head back with his eyes closed, reveling in every bit of this oral loving.

"Yo," Brian said to me, "my man is making a movie."

"I see," I said. Then I grabbed him by his pants and pulled him down the hall.

"Are you on camera fucking those girls?"

"Ah, no. Not yet."

"Are you on camera getting a blow job from them?"

"Well, maybe. But you didn't see my face."

I'm the guy trying to make Brian Barnes a sex symbol, so what's a little on-camera oral pleasure between friends? But it doesn't play like that. Even today, when MCs host porn tapes, which sell thousands, there's no place for hard-core sex in R&B. Okay, you got your R. Kelly tapes. But have you heard the R's *U Saved Me* CD? Even for the most raw, most sexually explicit, and painfully overexposed R&B singer of all time there's a time to put your clothes on. Brian Barnes was no R. Kelly, so he was even more vulnerable to scandal, humiliation, even blackmail.

So I walked over to "the set" and over to "the director/cameraman," where I engaged him in a bit of negotiation.

"What's your name, brother?"

"My name is Charles Brown, but people in the business call me Chilly Bone."

"Okay, Chilly. I'm Brian's manager, Dark—"

"Whoa, that's a great fucking porn name."

"Thanks for the tip, but I think I'll stick with my day job. And that day job includes protecting my client's career."

"Oh, man don't worry. I got your back. I won't use it."

"I know you won't 'cause you're selling it to me."

Chilly thought a moment. "That's cool. I hear you and

all. But you know I could really use an investor. It only takes about three thousand dollars to pay for this production, top to bottom. How's that for a, you know, accommodation?"

And that's how I became a partner in Chill Bone Productions. He'd "cast" his two "actresses" on the streets of the ATL. Shandi and Viv were two coeds from Morris Brown who had dreams of stripping at Magic City, the popular Atlanta strip club. They liked having sex and they had an affinity for big dicks. They were impressed by Lex's ample endowment. And it didn't hurt that Chilly Bone was paying hard cash.

Chilly was building a business of sex videos that recruited real girls to appear on camera and have raw sex. There had never been much black porn around when I was a kid, but camcorders and VHS tape was changing the game radically. I wasn't really interested in a long-term involvement, but I thought it wise to keep Chilly Bone happy.

So I wrote him a check and, that night, took Chilly, Brian, Lexington, Shandi, and Viv out to a soul food feast of fried chicken, black-eyed peas, potato salad, macaroni and cheese, big old buttered rolls, and iced tea so sweet it made my teeth hurt. The table was buzzing with the talk of parties. Everyone knew of a great party on Peachtree, which must be a kind of local joke since the town is full of thoroughfares named Peachtree.

After paying the check we ventured out into the mobile orgy. Cars were everywhere but they were in no hurry. They were all cruisin' like Smokey. Girls and guys hung out of car windows, convertibles featured brothers in tank tops or shirtless, flexing their biceps, hollering at females. Young women were in bikini tops and halters. Daisy dukes barely contained mountainous brown orbs. Girls jumped into cars. Girls tossed phone numbers. Boys tossed room keys. Girls pulled up their tops and displayed their titties. People prowled in a celebration of almost-naked black sexuality.

We rolled into a club on one of the Peachtrees where girls were participating in a wet T-shirt contest. Girls came out on a stage that protruded into the crowd. Bartenders sprayed their tops with beer. Boys struggled to catch the spillage from the girls' bodies. Nipples hardened. Dicks hardened. The 2 Live Crew boomed from speakers.

At a club on one of the Peachtree streets it was Mandingo night. Brothers in loincloths. Brothers with strings attached, brothers with chiseled muscles and six-packs in tight-fitting sacks, who grabbed girls. The girls happily grabbed them back. Lips smacked. Mouths opened. Girls squealed. People moaned. Girls attacked the stage. Security guards caught girls and swung them onto their hips like babies.

Around midnight I pulled Brian Barnes away from the crowd and said, "I don't know about you, but I'm all sexed out. You have a show to do tomorrow and I want you to blow everybody away. I know it's hard, but I want you to come back to the hotel with me and go to bed."

"You right," he agreed reluctantly.

"Remember: the more fans you have the more ass you get, and that's a fact."

My logic was inescapable. We bid our good-byes to our posse, promised tickets, and broke out. It took us a while to get through the hotel lobby, which was full of hoochies and wannabe shot callers. Brian's budding celebrity made wading through the lobby slow going, especially when girls were offering up their butt cheeks for autographing.

When I finally got Brian back to his room he sat on the sofa and fell asleep in seconds. I stretched him out, took off his shoes, and threw the top sheet from his bed atop him. It had been a busy day for my star. But tomorrow would be even more important.

Like a fighter before a championship bout, Brian Barnes paced around his small Omni dressing room. He threw punches in bunches. His feet moved in the wonderful rhythm of the gym. Every now and then he'd flick a jab at me but I ignored him. I was working the phone, fielding requests for interviews from newspapers and morning radio shows. Record stores wanted in-store appearances.

It was all happening. Everything had been on an upswing since Charlotte, but I still felt like the ATL would be another leap forward. Maggie had even called. Since our tour began I'd been in daily contact with Sony and my assistant at Plush, but this was my first conversation with Miss May since leaving New York.

"Looks like you picked a winner, Dark," she said. "Congratulations."

"He was a winner when I met him," I replied. "He just didn't know it yet."

"Can I speak to him?"

"Brian," I said, "my boss wants to talk to you."

He walked over, took my cell, and spoke confidently into the phone. "How you doing, sweetness? You miss me?"

I knew Maggie was eating it up 'cause after that Brian mostly listened. He say, "Yeah, that's right," and sometimes, "It feels good," but otherwise he was a mute witness to Maggie's praise. His last words to her were, "It's definitely gonna be special when I see you again" and then passed me back the cell.

"He's wonderful, Dark," she gushed. "He's everything you thought he could be."

"Eventually, he'll be even more, partner."

"Yes," she agreed, "partner."

As we were about to walk out toward the stage, an Omni employee walked up to me with a FedEx letter package. I signed for it and looked at the name. It was from Benita. I looked over my shoulder to see if Brian had noticed, but he was already walking toward the stage. I squeezed the FedEx in my hands. I walked slowly behind Brian. I saw a big garbage can. I ripped the FedEx package into three big pieces and then dropped them in garbage. If it got back to Brian I'd just say I must have left it in the dressing room. There was so much going on it was just an accident. By not reading it I could lie so much better if and when the time came. Ignorance is surely bliss when it comes to telling a convincing lie.

It wasn't the best show Brian Barnes had done to that point. The Charlotte show still held the crown, but the crowd was amazing, Horny, high, hyped up and happy, the Freaknik crowd was filled with carefree coeds, too-big-for-their-age high school girls, and lovely mature woman. They yelled and cheered at every one of Brian's pelvic thrusts, every falsetto riff, and every time he asked, "How you ladies doing tonight?!" or announced "Atlanta has the finest women in the country!" What got the loudest response of all? "Who's coming back to the hotel with me tonight?!"

Of course we weren't even going back to the hotel. We'd already checked out. The tour bus was full and waiting in the back. Right after Brian walked off the stage we were on our way to New Orleans. Freaknik had been great, but we had more extreme memories to make. Benita's FedEx made me frown, but the fact that she sent it was proof of how distant they'd become. I was in control. No worries. Not anymore.

chapter 12
Crescent City Redbone

Depending on the speaker and his or her point of view, the term "redbone" is either an apt description, an ignorant comment, or a high compliment. In the case of Brian Barnes, it was very much the latter. "Damn," he said as our tour bus cruised through lunchtime New Orleans, "I've never seen so many fine-ass redbone girls in my life!" Though some folks (perhaps some of my readers) might have a problem with "redbone," when you put "fine-ass" in front of it, well, you understand the young brother's intentions were good.

"Welcome to the Crescent City, Brian," I said, smiling as we looked out the window. "You've never seen women with complexions like these. Women with black, Indian,

French, and maybe a little Spanish, too, all of it creating mass confusion amongst the men folk. You heard of mulattos, right?"

"Interracial people?"

"Yeah. But down here they have all kinds of crazy science—quadroon, octoroon, and a couple of other categories I can't remember. All of it designed to measure how much nigga or how much cracker was in your blood."

"It's funny," Brian remarked, "that they made such a big deal out of it, since everybody must have been fucking everybody else to get it that mixed."

"Yeah, well, there were things that went on in the dark and things that went on in the light. At least down here people had to give a name to the nigga inside them. Most other places in America people practiced 'don't ask and we won't tell.' You're lucky, Brian."

"How's that, Dark? 'Cause I can have sex with all of them whatever name they use?"

"Something like that."

He turned and looked at me.

"You say that like that's not necessarily a great thing, Dark."

"Enjoy, but be careful, too. Keep that jimmy on tight. New Orleans is the kind of town that things happen in—things you regret and never forget."

"Something bad happen to you here?"

"No," I said, lying. "Nothing worth talking about. Nothing at all."

I didn't wanna burden him with my very personal New Orleans history. Back in '81 I'd come to the Crescent City for the first time, to attend the Black Radio Exclusive conference, an annual gathering of black radio and music executives sponsored by a weekly tip sheet news magazine. I was as green as a leaf and just real excited to be in the Big Easy on someone else's dime. A couple of acts I was comanaging were doing showcases. RCA Records was hosting a party for one of them; PolyGram was promoting the other. I was getting my first real props as an up-and-coming industry playa. I was really feeling myself, so when I stepped to a redbone beauty named Lucy in the lobby, I did so with gusto. She was a thin Creole lady, about twenty-one. The white sun dress with matching sandals made her bright red hair and red-toned skin burn my eyes.

The minute Lucy opened her mouth and a thick, French-flavored accent rolled out, I was in the palm of her small hand. I told her why I was in town and how much I wanted to see this legendary town like a native. She took me around New Orleans in my rental car. We went over by the Superdome, out to the Garden District, and to an incredible restaurant where I had to wear a bib to savor the big, oversize bowl of barbecued shrimp they plopped in front of me. All the while I whispered youthful sweet nothings in her adorable little ears.

Later, in my room, I ignored the faxes under my door and my blinking hotel phone message light. Instead I cracked open the minibar and plied Lucy with wine. But when my hands started to roam and my manhood started to rise, Lucy gave me a hard-core reality check: "I like you, Dark, but you'll have to pay."

"Pay? Pay for what?"

"It's two fifty to have sex with me. But only two hundred, for you 'cause you're so sweet."

"You're kidding. You're a prostitute?"

"An escort, mon cher. I hung with you 'cause I had some time to kill and 'cause you are real cute. But now I have to get paid."

I felt stupid. I felt played. I felt like a duck. "I'm not paying, Lucy—if that's even your name."

"Don't be mad, sweetie. I know I'm missing out. I really do. But if you're not paying I have to go now." She came over and kissed me lightly on the lips and then left the room. I sat in my room for a while, just cursing myself for being young, inexperienced, and everything else I could think of. When I pulled my ego back together and went down to the lobby, I saw Lucy sitting in the lap of a portly promotion man I knew named Lew. I walked by slowly, trying to catch her eye, but she was with Lew, deep in conversation with her new pal. I went back to the bar, ran into one of my acts, and made plans for the show later. Around 3:00 A.M. I saw Lucy again, this time holding hands with another promotion man. She saw me this time. She smiled. I just kept on walking.

Maybe my cynical view of sex and love and the

whole damn thing came out of that experience. Maybe I was just young. Misunderstandings between men and women happen every day over sex and commerce. Where are the lines between them? When is sex never about money or power? I thought about Tonique, the Philly singer/runner I was thinking of managing. I thought about Desiree, the Carolina beauty queen/actress who wanted me to guide her. I even thought of Shelly, the New York cocaine abuser/accountant who I'd given some business to. In each case there was a distinct economic element to our relationship.

Sitting in the tour bus, all my insecurities floated to the surface. It made me think of my ex-wife and how she'd left me. I really did crave someone to love me for me, but a road tour with a young R&B star wasn't really the place to find true love. More important to me was making Brian Barnes a star and myself a reputation as a starmaker.

I'd gotten feelers from a number of acts. Jody Watley had left a personal message at Plush's New York office for me. An attorney representing Alexander O'Neal had called. Word had gotten back to me that Tommy Mottola, head of Song Music and a former manager himself, had praised me in a staff meeting. So this wasn't the time to get all weak and sentimental. In fact, I needed to be more aggressive, particularly because New Orleans would offer a new test for Brian.

He'd be appearing as part of a weekend black music

festival at the Superdome sponsored by Budweiser. Luther Vandross, LL Cool J, the Whispers, Keith Sweat, Maze featuring Frankie Beverly, Al B. Sure!, and a few baby acts besides Brian Barnes would take the stage. It would be the first time many of Brian's peers would get to see him, so the show had to be right.

To that end I'd hired a real road manager to come on and micromanage the rest of the tour. With some tour support cash from Sony we were adding two female dancers and I'd had a backdrop designed with a Brian Barnes logo on it. At the hotel we were met by Bobby Duke, a veteran road manager who'd been out with Freddie Jackson, the Temptations, Melba Moore, and many others. Duke was a pro's pro who could handle everything from booking rooms to bailing out roadies.

Already checked in and having lunch at the hotel restaurant were our dancers, Le'shell Williams and Tosha Burt, who'd graduated from hip-hop clubs to become well-rounded show dancers. They were both lanky, fly, brown-skinned hotties who'd danced with LL Cool J and Lionel Richie. I was sure they'd enhance Brian's onstage sex appeal. And to make sure I was right, I'd hired Chi Chi, the woman who'd first brought Brian and me together, to come down and integrate the two dancers into the show.

Brian was overjoyed to see Chi Chi. So was I. In her own way, she was happy to see us, too. "So," she said, "you two managed to get a hit record." She spoke as if she couldn't believe it. Brian, Bobby, Chi Chi, and I went up to my suite and talked about where the show was and where it could go. Then we gathered up the band and the two dancers and rolled over to Tulane University, where I'd rented its student theater for a full-on rehearsal. Brian and the band ran through the show we'd been doing with Chi Chi watching. Afterward she marched up onstage and began moving people around. Homegirl was as forceful as she was sexy. A couple of times Brian bristled, wondering aloud why change was necessary.

At one point I pulled him aside and said, "Brian, we've been rocking clubs, but now we are starting to play bigger rooms. We need to add more visuals and more movement to play a place like the Superdome effectively."

He nodded reluctantly. I continued on. "Tonight we'll go to the Dome and you'll see what I mean."

After changing at the hotel, I rounded up my team and took them to an amazing restaurant, stuffing them with jambalaya, shrimp Creole, and enough rich food to put pot bellies on my two dancers. We got to the Superdome in time to see Luther Vandross. We sat on the floor of the huge arena. Brian's eyes surveyed the high ceiling and then the thousands of seats that surrounded us.

"This is bigger than Shea Stadium," he observed, more to himself than me.

"Yup," I said and cut Chi Chi a look.

"And once Luther takes the stage," Chi Chi added, "it'll feel like you're in his living room."

"Word?"

Word, indeed. Using three dancers, skillful choreography, amazing lighting, classy outfits, and, oh yes, the best voice in the business, Luther shrank the Superdome into an intimate little hall. Luther so moved me that I found myself holding Chi Chi's hand during his version of "Superstar."

"Oh," I said, about to take my hand away.

"No." She held me and then placed her other hand over mine. "It feels good."

Brian noticed this intimacy, smirked, but said nothing. After Luther and company left the stage Brian was gassed. "That shit was dope," he said.

"Well, we can't afford that level of production yet," I replied. "But we can start moving in that direction. We all need to get a good night's sleep and then do a blocking rehearsal tomorrow at the soundcheck, incorporating some of Chi Chi's suggestions."

"It sounds good—except for the good night's sleep," he said. "I saw you and Chi Chi and I think that's cool. But I'm feeling the need for some redbone, Dark."

"Okay," I said, "give me a half hour."

I called Bobby and put him on that mission. Then I stopped by Chi Chi's room. She opened the door and stood in the doorway. "Good evening, Dark. What brings you to my door?" In the background I could hear the voices of the two dancers talking and music playing from a boom box.

I replied, "You having a girl's night in?"

"We were actually thinking of hitting a club. You know Keith Sweat's on his way into town. He's getting in late and we may hook up with him and go out."

"Oh," I sad, quite deflated. "Well, I guess I wanted to see what you were doing."

"You could have called if that's all you wanted to know."

"That's true," I replied, now totally on the defensive.

"I liked holding your hand, too, Dark."

"Oh yeah?" I stammered a bit.

"And I'd like to do it again sometime."

"Just not tonight, huh?"

"Don't worry, Dark. Contrary to Keith's song, nothing lasts forever."

"Cool."

"Are you gonna go out with Brian?" she asked.

"We talked about it."

She leaned over and kissed me. When she pulled back I saw Le'shell peeking over her shoulder giggling.

"Oooh, I'm telling," she exclaimed and then we all laughed.

About an hour after that conversation I was in the back of a limo with Brian and Bobby, headed up a dark street lined with magnolia trees. The Gothic mansions had the grandeur of ancient money.

As we walked up toward the door, I asked Bobby, "Who told you about this place?"

"It's been here forever. From way back before integration," he said. "But I don't think they started letting black men in here until 1980 or something."

Bobby pushed the buzzer. You could hear the tinkling of chimes inside. A small window in the front door slid open and a pair of eyes gave my little posse the once-over.

"My name is Bobby Duke. I spoke to Madame Sinclair on the phone." The eyes looked at us a moment more and then the window shut.

"Shit," Brian said, "this is some drama, right here."

After a moment the door opened. The brother must have been six foot seven and two-hundred-fifty pounds. All squeezed into a tight-fitting tux. His name was Brockton and he guided us through a grand hallway with a long staircase and into a drawing room with a big fireplace. Oil portraits of elegantly clad white or Creole women decorated the dark wood paneling. On a table was a decanter of brandy and three glasses. Somewhere in the house was the sound of voices, but they sounded far away. We helped ourselves to the brandy and waited.

"Bobby, what have you got us into?"

In a whisper Bobby said excitedly, "My boys swear that this is one of the best—"

Bobby stopped talking when the door opened and a statuesque woman in a black satin corseted slip dress entered the room. What'd she look like? You've seen Vanessa Williams? Make Vanessa Williams sixty years old and that's who we met—a poised, smooth, high-yellow princess with a very regal bearing.

"Welcome, gentlemen. My name is Madame Sinclair and I am the manager of this leisure establishment. It will be a pleasure to help you enjoy all the pleasure you can stand." Each of us introduced ourselves.

When I took her hand I said, "I understand you have the best house of leisure in the city and we are honored to be here. These two men work for me and I want them to have the best you can offer. Money is no object."

"But what about you?"

"More brandy and some good conversation will make me happy."

Brian asked, "What? You ain't getting busy, Dark?"

"One of us has to be awake in the morning."

Madame Sinclair said, "Fine. Gentlemen, follow me."

We followed Madame Sinclair through a side door, down a short, dark corridor toward another wood door. We entered a room vibrant with life. The Meters's "Ai-PaKi-Way" flowed out of speakers. Flowers exploded out of ornate vases. Everywhere you looked were luscious red-, blonde-, and amber-haired Creole ladies. They lounged with drinks in their red-tipped hands. They slow danced with portly white men. They sipped drinks and chatted with very important-looking black gents in suits and ties.

"These are my ladies," Madame Sinclair said. "Take a look around and let me know who you'd like to meet."

Brian's eyes got big. It was like the idea he could have any of the women in the room completely over-whelmed him. "Damn," he said with a sigh, "they're all so fine, I don't know what to do."

Bobby, who'd been standing back silently, piped up. "Well, in my role as your new road manager, I'm ready to set up."

"Go ahead," I said with a smile. "Go to town, Bobby."

Within a few moments four Creole ladies eyed us—Helen, Francesa, Madaline, and Fefe. They were all dressed in clinging dresses and high heels with their hair arranged elaborately on their heads. "If you are satisfied with your selections," Madame Sinclair said, "the ladies will take you upstairs." Brian and Bobby, looking quite happy, were quickly escorted upstairs, while the madam took me by the arm and back through the corridor and into the first room we'd entered. Brockton stood behind a desk where a credit card machine had appeared. I handed my credit card to him and he ran it through.

As we waited she turned to me and observed, "Mr. Dark, you are a very disciplined man. Very few people, man or woman, walk in this establishment and don't find themselves indulging."

"A man has to have priorities," I replied.

My credit card cleared for three thousand dollars and then Brockton handed it back.

"I have a hard time believing you don't wanna spend time with one of my ladies."

"I guess I had a bad experience in New Orleans when I was younger and it's still very fresh in my mind."

She moved closer to me. "You're letting the past ruin your present? This place exists just so the past can disappear."

"For a little while."

"Isn't everything temporary, though?"

"You wanna please me, madame?" I asked. "Tell me a bit about your philosophy. I'm trying to train Brian Barnes to use sex as a tool. I bet you know a great deal about that."

She surveyed me for a moment and then picked up a glass and sipped some wine. Finally she said, "One manager to another?"

"Absolutely."

"You don't seem to need a lot of help when it comes to understanding sex appeal, Mr. Dark."

"Only a fool thinks he knows it all."

She took my arm and led me back into the main hallway and then up the long staircase, where a large portrait of Madame Sinclair hung at the top.

"It doesn't do you justice," I told her.

At that Madame Sinclair squeezed my hand and lead me down a long hallway. From closed bedroom doors I could hear the muffled sounds of pleasure and the rhythmic breathing that accompanies it.

We entered a room at the end of the hall. Inside were TV monitors, each capturing the activities in the bedrooms. The one central screen was off, but with the push of a button, it was filled with the image of Brian, Bobby, and the four red-toned employees of the madam cavorting in a four-poster bed.

"Looks like your friends opted for a tag-team approach," she observed wryly.

Bobby was on his knees, hands on his hips like a South American dictator, with Fefe and Francesa both feverishly sucking his rather unimpressive dick. He may not have had much, but he was enjoying what he had. On the other side of the bed was Brian. Now, he usually liked to sing when he screwed, but his mouth was full. Helen had her ample, red-haired pussy pressed hard against Brian's mouth as she stood over him on the bed. Down below Madaline was bent over the bed, sucking Brian's toes while working his dick with her hand.

"You don't look surprised," she observed.

"There's not much left that can surprise me about people's proclivities," I replied.

She began pointing to other screens, where various kinds of sexual activity—bondage, whipping, peeing, threesomes—were being vigorous enjoyed. "Well, if that's the case, there's nothing much I can tell you, Mr. Dark, 'cause that's the number one thing I've learned—never be surprised and never think you've seen it all. Every man and woman, employee or client, virgin or stud, comes into this house with ideas about what they'll do, what they'll like, and who they are in bed.

"But what they learn is that, especially in this city, any and all identities are situational. Every year Mardi Gras comes around, people put on masks and become more themselves than they ever knew. They fuck and they kiss and they suck and they bend and they thrust. All of which leads them far from who they were when they walked in the door. They may leave looking the same, but they never quite feel the same."

She turned back to the main screen and pointed. "Just look at what Brian has discovered about himself."

Brian's face was quite sweaty as he faced the mirror with his ass up in the air. Behind him was Helen, who with one hand was masturbating Brian, and with the other was probing his asshole with her lubricated finger. There was an open jar of KY jelly on the bed. Everyone else was gone. It was just Brian being explored by a woman with her fingers. The look on Brian's face was one of wonder.

Probably the same look was on my face. I think I'd spoken too soon about not being surprised. "So," I said after clearing my throat and turning away, "you provide your girls with an environment where being freaky is safe and lucrative, thereby getting them to see beyond fear and beyond their normal tastes."

"Are you a manager or a writer?"

"A manager. But one day I may write about you, Madame Sinclair. It must have taken years to put an operation like this together."

"And a lot of skill. It seems your young singer is back to being a missionary man."

Back in the bedroom, just on the other side of the mirror, there was Brian eating out Helen in a much more traditional exchange of fluids.

She asked, "Think I can get two tickets for the show tomorrow night?"

"I don't imagine that'll be a problem," I said and then I laughed.

"Mr. Dark," she wondered, "aren't you tired of watching?"

"I don't know, Madame. I told you I've been cursed in New Orleans. A Creole lady messed me up years ago. Since then, to be honest, I've never had sex in New Orleans."

"That's truly a sin, Dark, but lucky for you, removing curses is my specialty." She stepped close to me and took my hand.

Madame Sinclair's bedroom was draped in burgundy and gold, with candles, thick curtains, and layers of pillows and sheets all reflecting this lush combination of colors. She undressed me and I lay on my stomach as she poured some sweet-smelling oil on my back. Then I felt her tongue roll down my spine. The woman was old enough to be my mother, but her mouth and hands felt young as they explored the nooks and curves of my back, legs, and shoulders.

She turned me over and whispered, "I'm not finished" in my ear. I guided her on top of me and pulled down the top of the black satin corset that shielded her breasts from my eager hands. Her pointy breasts were the best that money could buy. I cupped them with my hand and squeezed the nipples with love. With a clever slight of hand the madam opened and slid a condom on my dick without seeming to move.

When our bodies merged, perfume filled my nose. She licked sweat off my brow. Her juices spilled down onto my groin. She held my head in her hands. My vision grew fuzzy. She was sixty or so years old and she could have uncorked a champagne bottle with her pussy. She was that good.

I left Madame Sinclair's with a list of guests for tomorrow night's show, promising a performance by Brian as good as the one her charges had unwittingly given us onscreen. We all fell asleep during the ride back to the hotel, a sweet slumber that was well earned.

The next day, rehearsals were outstanding. The edge was off Brian and he followed Chi Chi's lead. He didn't actually sing but walked through the songs and the steps. Offstage he and Bobby were chummy, a good sign since I was about to go back to the Apple to make some moves.

Chi Chi flirted with me all day. She kept asking what I did last night, and I was evasive at best. Brian and Bobby weren't as discreet.

"Naughty boy, Dark," she said.

"I didn't do anything," I replied. "I just watched."

"Don't treat me like a bald-headed stepchild," she said after sucking her teeth.

This banter went on right up to showtime. I was thankful 'cause it kept me loose. Brian, however, was unusually quiet before the gig. Part of it was simply playing the enormous stadium. Part of it was singing and interacting with the dancers. The final part was that he was coming on after Al B. Sure!, one of the new jack swing singers he was being compared to. It was his first head-to-head contest with a peer and he definitely felt the heat.

But he shouldn't have worried. First of all, Al bombed. I knew he only had a so-so voice, but Al was swallowed whole by the vastness of the Superdome. I'd have felt sorry for him except that it made Brian Barnes look like a seasoned pro. Chi Chi's stage tips, the new backdrop, and the addition of the dancers all combined to make Brian's show seem bigger and more sophisticated. He was no Luther Vandross, but he sure didn't seem like a rookie.

Afterward there was a serious crowd around our dressing room. Locals, as well as many of the pros from the world of R&B touring, came by to pay their respects. I pushed through the crowd, getting love from everybody for finding and managing the hottest new face in the game.

Then, in the dressing room, I saw something that I should have expected, yet it still fucked me up. There was Chi Chi, looking as radiant and sexy as ever, sitting in Brian's lap, whispering in his ear, and then giggling like a little girl. Le'shell and Tosha sat at Brian's feet, like purring cats awaiting a stroke from their master. Brian was official now. He had the look and aura of a star. Chi Chi's adoration was the final validation. It was what I'd been working for, but I wasn't happy. Not at all.

chapter 13
Big Apple Business

After New Orleans I went back to New York for three weeks. There was another deal on the table for Brian to appear in a Sprite commercial. There was an offer to have his version of "After the Dance" used on the sound track to an action flick starring Bruce Willis. Whitney Houston was planning a national tour and her agents were sniffing around for an opening act. I'd hired red-dress Shelly to supplement Plush's efforts and help Brian figure out what to do with his sudden pile of money. I'd kept our relationship strictly business, but felt she'd be loyal to me since I'd gotten her the gig.

There were several messages from Benita: "I need to

speak to you about Brian." "Brian is not returning my phone calls." With each message her tone grew both more desperate and angry.

After much internal debate I decided to call her. Luckily for me I just got her answering machine. Into it I simply said, "Benita, I am Brian's manager, not his message center. If you wish to speak to him, do so directly. I manage his career, not his love life. If you have issues with him that are personal, I don't have anything to do with that. I hope your career in medicine is going well. Thanks and take care."

So I shouldn't have been surprised when I walked out of Plush's office one afternoon and found Benita standing outside with a serious frown on her round face.

"Do you know what you've done?" she shouted.

"Excuse me," I said, trying to get her to lower her volume, "but I'm not aware of doing anything to you."

"Not to me, but to Brian. You've made him into someone as cold and empty as you are, as all you music business people are.

"I called Brian every day. I knew the minute I met you that your eyes were dead. I should cut you up like a coroner."

Heads turned. A few pedestrians slowed down. I must admit I was a little overwhelmed by her passion. I just replied weakly, "All I did was get him a record deal. It may not have been your dream, but it was his."

"His dream," she said, almost spitting the words, "was

to have a family. And he will 'cause I'm not gonna have this baby alone. Tell him *that*, Mr. Manager."

Whoa. I had no reply for that. I just stood there opened mouthed as Benita walked away. After I recovered I went back upstairs and called Yoli, enlisting her in a pact not to mention this information to Brian (I figured Benita would call her to get to him), so he wouldn't be distracted. Besides, this might be a ploy to get Brian's money (I didn't believe that, but Yoli did). Eventually Brian's dilemma would come out but hopefully not for a while.

I called Brian every day, never mentioning Benita. If he'd spoken to her himself he never let on. Our conversations were either strictly business or strictly sex. The midwestern leg of his tour was hitting seven more cities (Memphis, St. Louis, Little Rock, Milwaukee, Cleveland, Gary, Chicago), and I just wanted to keep his spirits up for that grind. Singing was now his business, no longer his dream. His new dream was the accumulation of sexual experiences. I pushed Benita out of my mind as he bragged about all the women he was screwing and how they were "feenin' for me." He told tales of being pursued by R&B divas, of being stepped to by the daughters (and the wives) of businessmen, and of groupies of every description. Brian Barnes had the Fever and his loins were inflamed.

I didn't ask about Chi Chi. I knew she'd been on and off the road with him since New Orleans and I knew she was still swinging with Keith Sweat, too. I didn't mention that to Brian, but I'm sure he knew about it and felt the heat of new jack competition. I wondered if either would win or would Chi Chi just roll on after declaring victory over both these would-be playboys.

As for my love life, it was in a period of flux. I'd hooked Tonique up with a Philly-based producer and had gone down twice to see her when I was in New York. Each time our visits were less about sex and more about music. I was now too enthralled by her voice to want that ass. Anyway, her boyfriend was still in the picture. A tall, lean, brown-skinned sprinter named Rob. I imagined he suspected something was up between Tonique and me, but he held his tongue. After all, I was paying for the demos.

And then there was Desiree Washington. I spent too much time watching her tape. She was so classy. So gifted. I wanted her, but she scared me. Desiree was different from Chi Chi, of course, but both women possessed a kind of internal strength that moved me. I fantasized at night of a woman who combined Chi Chi's brazen attitude with Desiree's poise. Then I'd masturbate furiously and fall asleep.

chapter 14
Lights Out

Though our relationship had evolved a lot since we first met—increasingly he saw himself as my employer and less as his mentor—he still rang me up in the wee hours with stories of his sexual exploits. It was like if I didn't know he'd done something freaky and fly, it really hadn't happened.

"Dark? Dark, you awake?"

"Now I am." It was 1:45 A.M. I hadn't been asleep but an hour or so.

"Good. I just had something happen you've never heard of before."

Now Brian was determined to stun me with some act or event I'd never heard of or experienced. It was a manifestation of our changed relationship. "Okay, my man, surprise me."

"So I came into the hotel after the gig. We'd stopped off and had dinner and drinks, but I'm telling you, I was dead tired. No ass for me tonight. I just needed to lay down."

"Been working you hard, huh?"

"You know that's right."

"So is there some sex in this story?"

"Can I tell it, please?"

"Come with it then."

"So when I get back to the hotel I get in the elevator. A woman yells, 'Hold it.' I press the 'open' button and this white woman gets in. Twenty-eight or so. Brunette. Looks a little Midwestern conservative but cute if she dressed better. Maybe she was some kind of young business-woman coming from a late dinner. You know, some-body's suburban girlfriend. She leans over to the buttons, sees that I pushed 12, and then turns and really looks at me and says, 'I know you.' I just nod. I'm tired. She doesn't look like a groupie and I'm surprised she even knows my music, but I'm not up for small talk. In fact I don't say a word to the woman.

"The elevator opens at 12. I pause to let her out first. I come out behind her. I turn left. She turns left. I go down the hall to my suite. I hear her walking behind me but don't think much about it. I don't figure she's gonna jack me, you know. Dark, you still there?"

"Yeah."

"Okay, so I go through my door. I open it and go in. I don't look to see it close. I just keep on walking. I walk straight across the living room right into the bedroom and just fall back on the bed, my clothes still on. I hear something. I look up and there the brunette is."

"Come on, Brian. You didn't hear her behind you?"

"The suite had a thick carpet, Dark."

"So what did you say?"

"Nothing. She just put her finger to her lips and then put that same finger to mine. Then she eased me back onto the bed. I just laid back. Homegirl unbuckled my pants and unzipped my zipper."

"No foreplay?"

"Nope. Nothing. She just went down there and took my dick in her mouth."

"Now that is strange."

"I told you Dark, this was some other type shit. I'm so tired I don't remember coming or anything else. I woke up right in that same spot on the bed with my dick hanging out and the girl gone."

"You check your pockets and your possessions?"

"Of course. My wallet was still in my pocket. So were my watches and my clothes. The only thing she'd done was write 'Good morning' in lipstick on the mirror with a big smiley face underneath it."

"No number?"

"No number."

"So, how does it feel to be a story?"

"She won't tell anyone what she did, Dark."

"You told me, right? Well, she didn't blow you like that just for the experience—she's telling someone, but not how you're telling it. I'm sure it'll end up the same way, with you asleep with your dick drying in the morning air, but I'm sure you'll have seduced her in the elevator or somehow been the aggressor. Either way, she'll have fruity drinks with a girlfriend and giggle about it every time your song comes on the radio while her husband or boyfriend is driving into a strip mall. She'll have that memory to smile about anytime she feels a little depressed or unsexy."

"Do you really think it's all that, Dark?"

"Yes, I do."

"Well go back to sleep then and have a nice dream because you're thinking too deep right now."

"I sure will get back to sleep. But could you do me one favor? From now on have security walk you to your door."

"I hear you. Good night."

chapter 15
Windy City Heels

I flew out to Chicago a few days before Brian's gig there in a last-ditch effort to get Brian Barnes on *The Oprah Winfrey Show*. I'd been calling. Our publicist had been calling. I'd even orchestrated a call-in campaign, hiring promotion people to call Oprah's switchboard demanding Brian get a chance to sing for her international audience. The best I could get from one of her producers was that she "might" come see him perform and, if properly impressed, that she'd give the Queen of All Media his CD.

It was quite frustrating. I just knew Brian's hunky, young black ass would make Oprah's heart go all aflutter. I even personally dropped off a bag full of promotional

CDs at her building, hoping the Big O would hear Brian's voice coming out of an office and wonder who that fine boy was.

As a consolation prize I'd gotten Brian booked on a local *Live at Five* news show with the highest ratings in the Windy City. I had also scored two prime seats for a Bulls playoff game. It was an attempt to rebond with my star after my three-week absence. But things didn't go as planned. The reason? Local newscaster Deniece Collins, thirty-five, on the dark side of cinnamon, with big, brown eyes and long, curly lashes. The Betty Boop effect of her face was accentuated by round, C-cup boobs, an unnaturally tiny waist, and appetizing hips that had more curves than an orange. Her mouth was okay, but that didn't matter since it was always open, either chatting with a local chef about a new recipe on the tube or laughing theatrically at life's little jokes.

When we'd walked into the station, Brian saw her picture on the wall and announced, "Oh, I'm gonna have that." It was a habit he'd picked up on the road. Lots of black entertainers (and I assume white boys, too) had gotten into the habit of going through fashion magazines to scout comely models or actresses. A manager or agent was promptly dispatched to find the girl, woo her with free tickets, a part in a music video, etc., and bring her to the horny celebrity.

It was a reverse gold digger move. Instead of the girl seeking out a famous man she'd read about, the star (actor, singer, or comic) now recruited the girl. In that spirit, Brian flirted with Deniece Collins on air, praising "the chocolate beauty of brown-skinned Chicago women" and how he "wouldn't leave the Windy City without a taste." Deniece, properly flattered and playing to the camera, flirted back. But once the red light went off she calmed things down, calling him a "nice young man" and "very sweet." These were signals that clearly said, "Look all you wish, but touching is prohibited." She then compounded the dis by, right in front of Brian, handing me her business card and writing her home number on the back.

"Let's have a drink before you leave town," she said.

"What about me?" Brian interjected.

"Oh," she said, "I really enjoyed having you on the show." Then she turned back to me. "Call me tonight? Okay?"

I answered affirmatively as Brian fumed. In the ride back to the old Nikko Hotel, my charge complained about Deniece's interview technique, her attitude, and her perfume. I just listened and nodded, all the while feeling her number burning a hole in my wallet. Even at the game, as Michael Jordan rained down jumpers and Scottie Pippen made a key steal, Brian bristled, as jealous of me for pulling a woman he wanted as I'd been of Chi Chi and him in New Orleans. Chalk it up to fair play, but in this case Brian Barnes had no interest in fairness. He didn't see me as a mentor anymore. Nope, suddenly I was a rival. That tension made both of us uneasy. It's dangerous for a manager to let a client get a chip on his shoulder when it comes to him. Artists are a volatile bunch and subject to making rash decisions.

Despite my concerns, I still had dinner with Deniece the next evening at Michael Jordan's restaurant. Over a very nice bottle of Cristal (charged to Brian Barnes, of course), we had a surprisingly frank conversation about her life and sexual predilections. In six Windy City years, Deniece had made a nice life for herself in the suburb of Oak Park. Her split-level home was a testament to gracious living, a place where she hosted two charity events a year and watched over three Siamese cats. To anyone who saw her on the air or read a profile of her in the local city magazine, Deniece lived a charmed life.

What was undercover was that Eric, her Morehouse-grad contractor husband, had left her for a white woman. This would simply be *Waiting to Exhale* territory if not for the circumstances surrounding this betrayal. Eric and Deniece had met Sheila Evans at a swingers weekend held at a rural resort in Indiana, and that embarrassment was compounded by the sad news that Deniece was bound to be childless unless she tried some costly and time-consuming fertility treatments.

After all that, there would be no more sharing of men or orgy action in her life again. "I've seen that movie," she said, "and I didn't enjoy the ending." Then she laughed her telegenic laugh that, in this case, was more a protective reflex than genuine amusement. I could tell she was actually still sad and shaken by how things had gone down. Why else would she open up so quickly to a stranger?

I told her I'd be leaving town the evening after our show at the United Center, but I could come back when the tour ended. "That's nice," she said, "but you do this thing for me and you won't have to see me again."

"What if I do, though?" I meant it. I could see myself drowning in those big baby-brown eyes.

"One thing at a time, Dark."

"What? Am I just a means to an end?"

"Same as I am for you." Then she added with some edge: "Besides, I don't see a gun being held to your head."

"Why me? This town is full of brothers."

"I don't really need to explain myself to you." She meant this. I knew if I pressed this point, Deniece might withdraw her offer. So I pulled back.

"Okay. I want you to be comfortable. However you wanna do things, it's all good."

She considered a moment and then said, "I have a very public job and I can't afford more talk. People are already wagging their damn tongues about my ex and me. A guy like you—good-looking, mobile, and with a little money—well, you have no reason to bust me. And just for the record, your singer was very sexy. But he was too young and seemed to have a big mouth. So are we through with all that?"

"Yes, we are. So what do you have in mind?"

Deniece talked about being in control and then, at some point, surrendering all that control. "Power mixed with submission and laced with discomfort—that's what I'm looking for," she said. "Not just a fuck. I want an experience. Perhaps a little theater. I majored in theater in college."

I got an idea for a game. She laughed when I explained what I wanted to do—this time with real amusement—and added a few touches. Right under a mural of Number 23 dunking we came up with a very different version of ball playing.

The night after the concert Brian and I stayed in Chicago an extra night before heading over to Detroit. I had a sedan take me out to Oak Park with a bottle of merlot. She ordered in Italian from a fine local restaurant. In her plush and relaxing living room we watched *9½ Weeks* and made out like teenagers on a deep, cushy sofa. My mouth was sliding between her beautiful breasts when Deniece announced, "I'm tired, Dark. The guest room is down the hall to the right." My dick was still hard as a ghetto winter. But no matter how much I begged she wouldn't give in. Following the script she marched me into a lovely guest room just off the kitchen.

I stripped down to my underwear and tank top, and laid on the bed. I didn't move. I just listened. Eventually a woman's high heels clicked against her parquet hallway. They walked over her bedroom carpet and clicked loudly against the tiles in her bathroom right above me. I looked up at the ceiling, listening and holding my increasingly aroused dick in my hand.

Slowly the heels got closer. In the hallway. Down the steps. Across the first floor. *Clop clop clop.* She took the steps in slow rhythm. I sat up in bed until she came into view. She sauntered past my door, no longer in her skirt or blouse, but in a bra, pantyhose, and stiletto heels. I could see her thick, black pubic hair as clearly as I saw her eyes.

"How are you?" I asked.

"Just getting some milk and cookies," she replied and then disappeared from view. Again I didn't move. I just listened as those lovely, sexy heels clopped across her kitchen floor. I heard the frigerator open. A cabinet door swung open and closed. Milk poured. Cookies crunched. The heels came toward me again. Deniece stood in the doorway. She had a chocolate chip cookie in one hand, a glass of milk in the other. There was a milk mustache across her top lip.

"Good night again," she said and then dipped the cookie in the milk and bit it square in half. She walked away and still I laid there. Didn't move a muscle now save my dick, which was quivering and ready. When I heard those heels going up the stairs, I leaped out of bed and dashed through the house, like a fox toward a rabbit. I came up behind her on the staircase, grabbed her by her hips, and buried my face between her pantyhose-enclosed ass cheeks.

She spread her legs while I twisted my head around, moving my tongue from her anus to her slit to her clit. On the tip of my tongue I tasted nylon, sweat, and pussy juice. Then milk, too, as Deniece poured what remained in her glass on my head. It was a strange brew but I was way past caring.

Deniece braced herself by putting her hands on the wall and railing. I used my two hands to rip a hole in her pantyhose. I put my face through that hole with her slit pressed around my goatee. She squatted, pressing her thighs around my head and pushing my body back against the stairs. Deniece now squatted so deep that my head was pushed back onto the steps, her pussy sitting square over my mouth and her knees on either side of my head. With a throaty moan Deniece came. Her legs shook. My mouth filled with an indescribable-tasting mixture of fluids.

Deniece climbed off my face and turned around so her face hovered over my lonely dick. At first she held it in one hand so that the tip was covered. She started licking my left testicle and then my right one, like snow cones. She spit—gooey and yellow—and placed the tip of her tongue at the base of my shaft. Using her spit as a lubricant, Deniece bent it back and slowly tickled it with her tongue, twisting around it but never reaching her mouth to my tip. Her fingers were long and soft and they followed her tongue up and around me.

As she sucked me I lifted my right leg and began rubbing it against her clit. In anticipation of tonight's activities I had had a pedicure, so my feet were soft and nails short. When I slipped my big toe into her slick pussy her butt rose up and shook. I felt her silky insides around my toe. It felt crazy to be doing this.

"You a little freak, aren't you, Dark?"

"Takes one to know one," I replied and then pulled my toe out. I slid from under her and pulled her by the shoulders, pushing her front against the wall. I stuck my left index finger inside her pussy and then crooked it, so that it created a gentle roughness in her. I followed that with my middle finger, linking them together like one slender dick for several stokes before splitting them apart, letting them roam around inside Deniece while my palm rubbed against her clit.

"What are you doing?" she said.

"Finger-fucking that sweet black pussy," I said in her ear with a leer.

"Do you wanna fuck me?"

"No 'wanna' here, baby. I am fucking you. Now if you want my dick instead of fingers, you gotta beg for it."

"No," she said. I pushed my fingers deeper in her. Again she said, "No." I made my hand into a fist inside her and pushed her face against the wall with my other hand.

"Beg, bitch! Beg for my dick!"

"Ah," she moaned. "I want your dick."

"You want what, bitch?!" I shouted. "You want *what?!*"

"I WANT YOUR DICK!"

From inside her ripped pantyhose she pulled out a condom, so she definitely still had her wits about her. I put it on, using my teeth to rip the package open. Once in place I put my condom-covered penis up into her wetness. Felt like I was entering an oven.

After all that foreplay we were both ready to fuck like animals. This wasn't about lovemaking. I stood behind her and pumped away. Her walls were loose from my hand and fingers, so I squeezed her cheeks together. Then I got a nasty idea. I reached down and scooped her pussy juice up around her asshole. With no warning I pulled out and then began rubbing my dick against the opening of her asshole.

Deniece just moaned and arched her back. I slid the tip in and she made a wild, guttural sound. Her left leg came up and she bent her right leg, sticking my leg and then my ass with it as I pushed deeper inside her anus. Now she screamed—really loud and intense. The tightness of her butt, the way her body shook, and my own amazement at being that far inside her all combined into her deep, almost painful orgasm. It felt like the sperm was being pushed out slowly, one drop at a time. I pulled out and fell back onto the steps.

My condom was covered with pussy juice, shit stains, and even a bit of what looked like milk. I just stared at it and breathed heavily. Only then did I become aware of the bruises on my ass, my back, and even my neck from the stairs. Deniece stood over me, rubbing herself be-tween the legs.

"Your cheeks sore, Dark?"

"Hell yeah."

"A little pain is good for the soul. It lets you know you're alive."

I slowly pulled the condom off me. A little semen spilled out onto her stairs. "Well," I replied, "I must be living well then."

Back at the Nikko I was prepared to enjoy a very good night's sleep, but it was not to be. Bobby left a voice message telling me that Brian had a lunch meeting that afternoon with reps for Hush Management, the folks who handled Freddie Jackson, Kashif, and several other suc-cessful R&B acts.

I walked right over to Brian's room, let myself in, and, to my surprise, I found him sitting on his sofa with Shelly, the cocaine-loving business manager from New York. Her eyes were red. Papers were on the cushion next to her.

"Shelly," I said, trying to hide my discomfort at her presence, "when did you get out here?"

Before she could answer, Brian cut in: "I brought her out. Just wanted to see how my money was flowing."

"Is that right?" I said. "Is there some problem you wanna ask me about?"

"It's all in order." This was Shelly, finally opening her

mouth. "Really. I actually reached out to Brian myself. I thought it was important he know me since I've been handling a lot of his money."

Now I was mad and didn't try to hide it. "Well, let me be frank. I don't like meetings like this being held behind my back. If there's a meeting like this to be had, I should be made aware of it. Is that clear?"

"Motherfucker," Brian said with a raised voice. "You work for me. Don't forget that. Shelly works for me, too. I'm the one the women scream for. I'm the one who works that stage. I'm the one who sells those tickets. It's time you stopped treating me like a kid."

Brian had never talked to me like that before. I was kinda stunned. I was definitely hurt. I wanted to walk out of the room. I wanted to kick his ass. Instead, I said, "Look, Brian. You are right that I work for you. You have every right to check on your money. But remember that trust is the only bond that truly matters in this business. You have to trust me. You also have to know that the happier you are, the better I look to the world. All I ask is don't disrespect me and I won't disrespect you."

"Yeah," Brain said. He sounded reluctant to acknowledge my point.

Shelly piped up. "Would you guys like some coke? I happen to have some in my purse."

"No thanks," I said.

"You get down like that, baby?" Brian asked.

"From time to time," she answered.

He looked at her curiously. "Okay," he said. "Well, I'm gonna get some sleep. We heading out in the morning and my manager's got me doing some early-ass radio interview. We'll talk more in the morning."

Shelly left with me and came dutifully down to my room. Soon as the door closed I peppered her with questions: "Okay, why didn't you let me know you were in town?"

"It was very last minute and he wanted it hush-hush. It *is* his money, you know?"

"What did Brian wanna know? Does he think I've mismanaged his affairs?"

Shelly swallowed hard and then replied, "He wanted an update on what you were commissioning and how much you were earning. He wanted it confidential. He thinks you're doing a good job, but—and you won't like this—he's been fielding offers from other managers."

Jealousy about a woman choosing me over him. Flying in people to check up on how I did business. Meeting with other, more established management companies. It all pointed to big problems down the road.

Right along with the Fever came a deep sense of entitlement and a growing sense of paranoia. The star believes he should have whatever he wants and anyone who says otherwise or, God forbid, stops them is suddenly suspect. They begin collecting men and women who tell the star what he wants to hear, people who slowly isolate them from reality. It's as if the sexual license of stardom begins to eat away at their sanity. This is the darkest side of making a star. You never know who's whispering in their ear or what they're saying. Soon you are as fearful as they are and get wrapped in a cocoon of anxiety.

Shelly, I could see, was helping create that cocoon for Brian. She laid a line of cocaine out on a table for me. I told her to leave and then watched as she scooped the cocaine back into a vial with the care of a detective brushing for prints.

I looked out the window. The river that led to Lake Michigan flowed below me. The wild night with Deniece seemed so long ago. I called Tonique. I called Desiree Washington. I made plans. I thought about Los Angeles, which was just a few days away, and wondered if my relationship with Brian Barnes would survive the City of Angels.

chapter 16
My Momma Said

What did you do?"

It was 5 A.M. in the morning. Our flight from Chicago to L.A. was at 9, so I wasn't expecting my wake-up call for another ninety minutes. But this wasn't the front desk. It was Brian, who sounded both a little drunk and quite wide awake. This wasn't like one of our previous calls when he'd awakened me to brag about a new sexual adventure.

"Could you be more specific?"

"My mother just called me from New York real upset. Apparently the limo driver broke up with her."

"That's what you wanted, right?"

"Yeah, but it seems like it went down funky."

"How was that supposed to go down good, Brian? He was using her to try to get some of your paper. I hate to put it this way, but he had her open, right? You wanted it handled, so I handled it."

"You are always manipulating people, aren't you, Dark?"

"Did you want that situation to go away or not? Part of what you're paying me for is to make your life easier. That's what I did."

"Well, I did want her to stop bothering me about investing in a business she didn't know jack about. But she says she's lonely and she's bad at being lonely."

"What? Now you want me to find her a boyfriend?"

"You would, wouldn't you? You'd just make a couple of calls and a man would appear at her door. You'd do her like you do me."

"You are really a little extra this morning, Brian. Well, let me lay it out for you. I hooked the man up with a new limo company where, if the driver brings his own car, he would be offered a big of equity in the business. It's a way to insure top-quality service. I didn't explicitly tell him to stop dating your mother. I just told him that to make this work he'd have to devote himself to the gig. I happen to have a piece of the company myself, so I said I'd be monitoring his work habits. More time behind the wheel meant more money for him and less time with your mother and, to be frank, less need for your mother. I figured eventually it would change their relationship."

"How come you didn't tell me any of this?"

"You've been kinda busy singing and fucking your way across America. You been blowing up like nitro, Brian. That's what you've been focused on and that's the way it should be."

"Everything is a secret with you, Dark, you know that? You always got agendas. Things are going on around me that affect me, but it's like I'm just a spectator in my own damn life. This is my life, Dark."

"I got secrets? I'm not the one who's got a coke fiend accountant gong behind my back. Who was secretive there?"

"It is my money."

"No argument there. But I think our business relationship has benefited you and benefited me and good business, like love, is built on trust."

"Dark, come on with that love shit. You don't love anyone. And I know better than to get caught up in a love thing right now. You have shown me that. It's like they want to suck all the energy out of you, like I'm a damn battery. I'm human too Dark. How come people don't treat me like that anymore?"

"You know how people get sad and feel they're a failure? Well, success can make you sad, too. Too much pussy can mess you up as much as not enough. But you'll get used to it. After a while, it'll feel as natural as bottled water."

"Is that a joke?"

"Bottled water is real water. It's just a little more protected and a little safer than what comes out of the tap.
For you I'm that protection."

"You sure can talk shit, Dark. I wake your ass up and
out it pours."

"You ready for L.A.?"

"I guess. Ma and Yoli will be out there, so I gotta
hang with them a bit. That'll either calm me down or
drive me crazy."

"You packed?"

"Kinda."

"Well get to it then. I got plans for you out there,
Brian."

"You always seem to, don't you? See you in a
minute."

"In a minute."

chapter 17
Angelic Behavior

Brian Barnes had never been to Los Angeles before and the part of him that still wasn't a star really wanted to be a tourist. He wanted to place his feet in the footprints of old Hollywood stars in front of Mann's Chinese Theater and have his picture taken in Beachwood Canyon with the Hollywood sign behind him. It was that innocent side of Brian that led him to fly out his mother and sister and put them up in a suite at the Beverly Hills Hotel.

But there was a newly emerging side to Brian, the one I'd cultivated and nurtured. The side that was a multiple Soul Train Award nominee (Best Single, Best New Artist, Best Male Singer). That side of him only wanted to have lunch at the Ivy on Robertson and hang out at the Roxbury on Sunset, which was blazing hot at the time. It was that new side of Brian that booked a bungalow at the Beverly Hills Hotel, giving him a private entrance where he could do dirt away from his family's prying eyes.

And I was there when those two warring sides of my young star, at once innocent and newly jaded, came into conflict. We were at a posh boutique on Beverly Hills' Rodeo Drive. I stood on the side observing Brian, Yoli, and his wild ass mother, Jezebelle, who was in the process of buying her first designer dress. Like kids with a twenty-dollar bill at a candy store, the Barnes women were trying on dress after dress, running the saleswomen ragged. They weren't being divas—just indecisive, wide-eyed, and overwhelmed by having so many pricey options.

My role was to reassure the slightly stuffy staff that these three had the cash to purchase their final selections. This was before the era when rappers became regulars at designer shops, so the sales staff was courteous but skeptical about this trio's buying power.

But they suffered no financial anxiety when Whitney Houston, her mother, Cissy, and a bodyguard entered. I'd been introduced to Whitney a couple of times, so neither she (nor her security) were freaked out when I walked over. Homegirl even gave me a kiss on the cheek.

When I brought Brian and family over to meet her it was a real lovefest. Jezebelle pulled out her Instamatic camera. Whitney and Cissy posed for pictures with the Barnes clan, and seemed to really enjoy Jezebelle and didn't seem to mind the intense hugs. It was a working-class black woman's moment to bond with a star and it was great to see.

Brian, in sad contrast, seemed a little piqued to have met Whitney Houston this way. Instead of being the center of attention, he had to share Whitney with his mother and sister. At one point he whispered to me, "I've waited for years to meet Whitney and now she'll remember my mother more than me."

I reassured him, saying, "At least she'll remember you with a smile." That didn't do much to make him happy, especially when Yoli and Jezebelle began getting clothing tips from the Houstons that increased his shopping bill from three thousand to seven thousand dollars.

That evening Brian hired a limo to take Jezebelle and Yoli out to the Universal Studios theme park, while we rolled over to L.A.'s club du jour, the Roxbury. The spot had three levels; a ground-floor bar, a second-floor restaurant, and a third-floor disco with a heavily guarded VIP room that had a private entrance. This VIP room was a magnet for stars of both the A- and B-list variety, and groupies and hangers-on of every damn description. It was a place where the fruits of celebrity were plucked from very low-hanging trees.

I struck up a conversation with Senna, a dark brown sister with thick, straight hair and a very flattering green, low-cut dress. Turned out she worked as the accountant for a Beverly Hills plastic surgeon and was rolling with two big-breasted blondes, L.A. Raiders cheerleaders named Orline and Marsha. With Senna and her two friends in tow I commandeered a booth. I was vibing Senna and Brian was drinking with the Raider girls when Rick James walked over to the table.

"What's up, youngblood," he said to Brian, who rose to shake his hand.

Rick James was a fixture in the Roxbury's VIP room, usually rolling in around midnight to scoop up a ten-deroni or two. It was known that Rick kept a room at the St. James Club, an Art Deco hotel a few blocks away, for various nocturnal activities. I heard talk that Rick was getting crazy with the crack pipe. That night, however, the original Slick Rick was charming as hell, telling us stories of Marvin Gaye and the glory days of Motown.

A crowd of folks had gathered around our table, jocking the king of punk funk and my new jack swing star. Brian was so happy. "Can you believe this?" he said several times, just tripping on being down with the ultimate superfreak. Rick told us to meet him at a Soul Train party being held at a Century City spot called R&B Live.

R&B Live was the hottest black party in town, a place with a live band that allowed unknown singers to perform in jam sessions with big-name artists. We were gonna check it out anyway, but rolling in with Rick James would have been some cool-ass rock 'n roll shit. I kept Senna with me, while Brian and the Raiders girls wanted to squeeze in with Rick. My better judgment outweighed my excitement, so I made a reluctant Brian ride with me. Not surprisingly the two Raiders girls went with Rick.

Well, we got out to Century City in one piece, but Rick (surprise) didn't show up. Brian was pissed and disappointed. He barked at me for not letting him travel with Rick but, considering Rick's well-earned rep for extreme drug use, I knew I'd done the right thing.

Once we'd entered R&B Live Brian's spirits lifted considerably. Shalamar's Howard Hewitt was onstage, doing a loose rendition of his classic "For the Lover in You" accompanied by a seven-piece band. The booths were filled with R&B royalty: Stevie Wonder shaking his head at one table; Arsenio Hall chatting with Paula Abdul; and at a serious power table there was Eddie Murphy and Prince talking as Sheila E. tapped her hand in time to the music. Somebody said Anita Baker was in the house but I didn't see her.

"Yo, Dark, you gotta get me onstage." Brian was very excited. "I gotta blow for these folks." I found the light-skinned, wavy-haired dude who ran R&B Live and kicked the ballistics. New jacks wanting to blow for free was what the club featured, so they were overjoyed. I shuttled back and forth between Brian and the bandleader, a cool keyboard player who played and chatted at the same time.

When Brian hit the stage the band flowed into a funky version of Marvin's "Got to Give It Up." The groove was thick and Brian floated over it like a cloud. And it got even better when Stevie came onstage and got behind the electric piano to guide Brian through a righteous version of "Higher Ground."

Afterward I was exchanging numbers with Stevie's brother and talking with the musicians. Everyone was impressed with Brian. Even I found new respect for him. He handled the star power in the room by going out and commanding their respect. He hadn't been timid or intimidated. His newly found arrogance might have peeved me at times, but it was also translating into a mature confidence in his abilities. Couldn't be mad at that.

Around 2:00 A.M. we ended up at somebody's mansion in the Hollywood Hills. There were stars, friends of stars, managers and agents of stars, and wannabe friends of stars. And a spectacular view of the city spread out before us. There were people in the Jacuzzi. There were people in the pool—some with clothes on, some with swimming outfits, and one brazen man buck naked.

A haze of marijuana smoke hung in the living room as thick as the city's midday smog. The miracle of the night was that Senna was still with me. Despite all the stars we'd encountered and my busy networking, this dark beauty had hung with me. She held my hand and cuddled against me as we pulled on a joint a Soul Train dancer passed my way. Brian had disappeared into the crowd but I was too mellow to worry.

Through the living room's glass window I spotted Chi Chi and, of all people, Maggie from Plush, sharing champagne on the deck. Maggie had not talked about coming out for the Soul Train Awards, so I was not happy to see her here, knowing she hadn't called me. Moreover, she looked awfully chummy with Chi Chi and I wondered what that meant. For a minute I almost pulled my hand out of Senna's but then caught myself. I didn't owe Chi Chi a thing she hadn't been paid for, so no need to be self-conscious. She was a free agent and, damn right, so was I.

Senna tapped me on the shoulder and pointed across the room to a stairway, where Brian was following—would you believe it—Rick James and the Raiders cheerleaders upstairs.

"That looks like a potentially freaky situation," Senna said.

"Is that a good thing or a bad thing?" I wondered.

"Well, I know those Raiders girls and I've heard all about Rick's activities. It might not be what you want your client all up into."

"Really?"

"Listen," Senna said, "I love a good time as much as the nice girl, but Rick goes too far."

"You are a very levelheaded and beautiful woman, Senna."

"Baby, I work for a Beverly Hills plastic surgeon. You can't believe what I've seen."

"I bet. Let's get out of here."

"I'm with that," she said, then added, "But you really should look in on Brian. He seems young and nice. You might save him some trouble."

I was a little embarrassed that a plastic surgeon's accountant was schooling me on protecting my artist. We walked hand in hand up the staircase where we found three bedrooms and three closed doors. Knocking on the doors at a Hollywood swingin' party didn't seem like a good idea. I stood there a moment, considering whether to put my ear to each door like a snooping neighbor, when Brian came out of one of the rooms looking wide-eyed and very agitated.

"I was coming to tell you we're going," I said as he came toward us.

"I'm going with you," he said and then brushed past us. Gray smoke emanated from the bedroom he'd just escaped. There was the sound of a man's manic laughter. A white woman's hand closed the door.

"What happened?" I asked Brian.

He just kept walking and said over his shoulder, "You don't wanna know and I sure don't wanna remember."

During the ride back to the Beverly Hills Hotel, Brian sat in a corner of the limo, as quiet and withdrawn as I'd ever seen him. I decided this wasn't a good night to leave my client alone, so I sent Senna home to

Culver City in the limo (which I considered a major sacrifice) and sat up in Brian's bungalow and shared black coffee. We didn't say much. Mostly we listened to tracks that had been submitted for his next album, giving thumbs-down to most and maybes to a few. We sat up talking music until 4:00 A.M. It took him that long to loosen up.

"Yo," he said, "I sang with Stevie Wonder tonight."

"That's right, Brian, and you sang your ass off."

"And I saw Rick James. I saw him do his thing. That crack rock controls that nigga, Dark."

"Yeah, it's the downfall of so many."

"Yo, Dark, he had a pipe and made those Raider girls hit with him. I guess that's what they went and did. After that they'd do whatever Rick wanted them to. Fuck him. Fuck each other. Stick shit up they ass. Damn, I've been in some orgies recently—"

"Yes, you have."

"But the vibe was just foul, Dark. Felt like the devil was in the motherfucking house."

"Too much sex. Too many drugs. Too much money, but no respect for it. If you're not careful, if you're not grounded, you'll end up just like Rick James."

Then, out of left field, he asked forcefully, "You wanted me to let Benita go, didn't you? From even back when we all first met that night at the Apollo."

"That wasn't an actual goal," I said, clearly lying. "Girlfriends always get dumped. But they often come back. Often stars find that their original lover is the only person they can actually trust."

"You know," he said, looking at me hard, "you kinda a devil yourself."

I tried to laugh it off, like I knew Brian was joking, but he wasn't. "Every man's got a little devil in him, Brian. You know that."

"I just wanted to sing. I wanted to be famous, yes. But you broke me down like a pimp does a ho."

"Come on, Brian. That's not—"

"She had an abortion, Dark."

"Ah . . . when?"

"Over the summer. A couple of months ago. Said she tried to call me, but my numbers were changed. Said she sent me a letter way back when we were in Atlanta and that you signed for it."

"I don't remember that, Brian."

"Neither do I. A lot of this summer is a blur." He stared off into the distance. "Yoli finally broke down and gave her my new number. We spoke the other day. Been thinking about this summer. Didn't know what I thought, you know. I was sad, but I didn't think it was my fault. Then I saw Rick James and thought of his life and all the motherfucking pain he must have inflicted and all the pain he must have inside because of everything he's done to people."

"You're not Rick James, Brian."

"Not yet." He looked over at me, his eyes teary and

heavy. "And, you know, you are at the center of everything that's happened, good and bad. I'm not sure I would have told Benita to keep the baby."

"Probably not," I said, trying to regain control by being hyperrational

"But it was *my* decision to make. Now I'm thinking you made it for me and you made it for Benita by keeping us apart."

"Brian, that . . . that's crazy."

"GET OUT OF MY ROOM!"

"What!"

"GET THE HELL OUT, MOTHERFUCKER, BEFORE I KICK YOUR OLD ASS OUT!" Brian was standing over me now with clenched fists. I stood up and looked him the eye.

"Just get some sleep, Brian. We both need some sleep."

He yelled at me again—-a bunch of obscenities—and I walked out of his bungalow at the crack of dawn. Obviously I didn't sleep well. The Soul Train Awards were the next day and we had meetings scheduled with TV and film people. Would he come? Would he fire me? About 10:30 the next day I was awakened by the hotel phone and a welcome voice on the other end of the line.

"Good morning. Guess who's in town?" It was Desiree Washington. I pulled myself together, jumping in the shower and pouring a bottle of Visine on my eyes, and walked down to the Polo Lounge, where the most beautiful woman in L.A. sat waiting on me.

"Dark," she said sweetly, "you look terrible."

"And I feel worse than that." Then I did something quite out of character. I was honest with her about how I'd handled Brian and what I'd planned and talked about my post-break-up behavior (though not in the nasty detail I've told you here).

Desiree listened carefully and asked, "If you're so bad, why were you such a gentleman with me in North Carolina?"

"You carried yourself with a lot of class. Simple as that. Plus you had talent and I respected it and you."

"And I had a boyfriend."

"Listen," I said in reply, "if I'd really wanted you, he wouldn't have mattered."

"You really can sound like an asshole, Dark. I see that now."

"I know. But humble niggas don't get any respect in this game. Black men had to be professionally humble for years. I don't have to, so I won't."

She just laughed at me and shook her head. Then she took my hands in hers. "You're so self-absorbed, you didn't even ask me why I'm out here."

"Okay. You're right. I haven't used the manners my mother taught me."

"I got invited to go to the Soul Train Awards with

Keith Sweat." Turns out she'd met Sweat during her sickle cell work at Tubby's and he'd wisely kept in contact with her.

"That square-headed boyfriend of yours is going for that?"

"We broke up," she said. "He was too controlling. I had to move on. I'm also moving out here. Got a place in an area they call Culver City. So, no, Keith didn't fly me out here, nor is he paying my room and board."

"We've been talking. You didn't tell me any of this. You have more game than I thought. But there's no way you're going to the Soul Train Awards with Keith Sweat."

"You my daddy now?" she said with mock indignation.

I just leaned over from my chair and kissed her. At first she pulled away, but my lips were insistent and she yielded to me, making her mouth firm and gentle. "I'm not gonna fuck Keith Sweat, Dark. But I will make him look good at the Soul Train Awards. I'll meet a lot of people. I'll begin setting up my career. But I do need a manager and I do need a man."

"I'm not a good choice," I said honestly.

"I've never had a man turn me down before. Wow, it kinda turns me on."

On that tour in the summer of 1990 I'd had sex with all kinds of women in all kinds of situations. But that afternoon, though I was tired and a little depressed, I had the best sex of my life. Desiree's body spread out before me—firm and brown and curvy and soft as cotton. I ate her, savoring her tangy, supple flavor and then swallowing her essence, taking Desiree inside me. I was so hard and anxious I thought I'd come in moments.

But Desiree must have sensed my anxiety, 'cause she guided me in carefully, gripping me inside her. It felt like I'd dipped my dick in a vat of cocoa, sweet and warm.

She took me in, rolling her hips like a belly dancer, flicking her lips like a snake in my right ear. One hand cupped my ass. Another clutched my head. We looked into each other's faces and said each other's names as we moved together, validating each other's efforts with our gaze.

To make love to someone as gorgeous as Desiree Washington can seem like a dream. But our lovemaking was hard and real, as gritty as dirt and impactful as a fall. I held nothing back. No part of me was not engaged—my dick, my head, my heart. I was right there with Desiree, smelling her perfume, her sweat, and her pussy. And every smell made me hard again. So hard I thought I'd never come again, just stay perpetually hard in her presence.

When I woke up it was 4:00 P.M. I'd missed meetings. I'd missed phone calls. I'd missed soundcheck. None of it mattered. None of it.

"You know you're not going anywhere with Keith Sweat."

Desiree smiled. "Yeah. That's probably not a good idea at this point."

We ate room service, fed each other in bed, and finally showered, rubbing clean all the sour parts on our bodies. I gave her my ticket and the limo and told her I'd meet her at the awards show. I had to go confront what I assumed would be a still furious Brian Barnes. I walked over to his bungalow, ready for whatever. I was about to knock on the door when I heard familiar grunting and sucking.

I let myself in. Clothes scattered on the floor. A champagne bottle. The smell of herb. Coke on a tray. I missed a real party, it seemed. The bedroom door was open. Inside, the bed was full. Brian lay on the bed, his face obscured by a pillow. I could hear Brian singing a muffled "Distant Lover." In the middle of the bed was Maggie, my boss, in some very tasteful La Perla lingerie, blowing our client with gusto. Next to her was Shelly, who was snorting coke off Brian's leg, her nostrils as red as the garter belt and heels that were the only items of clothing on her narrow body. Neither woman saw me as I backed out into the living room.

Then I almost jumped out of my skin when someone grabbed my ass. Chi Chi stood there holding a bucket of ice and wearing nothing but a white camisole, like a member of Vanity 6. "Where have you been?" she asked. "Your client has been looking for you all day. Maggie was looking for you, too. Thank God I was here to cover for you."

"You made this happen, didn't you?"

Chi Chi laughed. "I do have that ability, Dark. You know that."

"Did he fire me?"

"He kept flipping between firing you and apologizing for the way he spoke to you. I made sure he came to the right conclusion. After all, I am your partner. I gotta look out for our interests. Besides, have I told you how proud I am of you?"

"Proud? What? Are you my mother now?"

"No. I'm not trying to be anything like that. I'm just saying I may have turned you onto Brian, but you molded that material. You got your hustle on and made it happen."

"Thank you," I said, "but I know there's more, Chi Chi."

"Well, Maggie told me she's gonna finance an expanded black music management biz with you running it. I wanna continue our business relationship. I wanna run artist development—from styling to dancing to talking to the press. I've been around the game for a long time. Now it's time I cashed in."

"Maggie told you all that?"

"As you can tell, I kinda have her confidence."

"You're a bad dick bitch, Chi Chi. No doubt about that. Sure," I said, "if this goes down, you're with me."

She reached over, pulled me close, and tongued me with a dancer's grace. After a long, lingering kiss, she said, "You in a mood to negotiate terms?"

"I think I've just fallen in love with someone." This made her laugh hard. "Come on. You don't believe I can fall in love?"

"No," she said, after pulling herself together. "Anything can happen, I guess." Then she shook her head and added, "But we have a bond, too, Dark. Always remember that." Then she took her melting ice cubes and headed back into Brian's bedroom.

I'd like to say that the Soul Train Awards ended a wild few days on a note of triumph for Brian Barnes, but I'd be lying. The real people in the upper reaches of the balcony Soul Train Awards audience like to act like they were at the Apollo Theater. In the past they'd booed Whitney Houston, Mariah Carey, and they'd later get all over Ashanti.

So when Barnes came up and did a Marvin Gaye classic and was a little hoarse and, because he was hoarse, sounded a bit off key, several folks in the balcony booed him. Wasn't a lot of people. Three, maybe four, but you could hear them. Barnes did. He looked unsettled onstage. Not the confident stud I'd been cultivating for a whole summer. Moreover, Brian Barnes didn't win a single Soul Train award. Shut out completely.

In the limo to the official after party I took stock of my situation. I still had Brian under contract with Plush. Whatever move he made next I'd get a piece of his pie. Building a second album would both be easier since he was now known, and harder since it would be compared to the first. Someone else should run that show. Maggie had empowered me to expand. It was time for me to find another star. I was hot now myself. And I was going to move into hip-hop. That's where the energy was. That's where it seemed you could go pop in a massive way.

At the party Desiree introduced me to a young director named John Singleton. He was just out of USC film school and there was a lot of heat on his script about some homeboys from South Central. He was about to start shooting soon. Said I should look into West Coast rap. There were young directors coming up in Hollywood and the local rap scene was blowing up with NWA and Ice Cube. Black Hollywood and ghetto hip-hop were mixing together. Seemed like a smart brother could make money out here. But that's another story.